Cash Only:

A Hoe Cartel

TY NESHA

Queen of the Hill Publishing
LAKE FOREST, ILLINOIS

NOV 16

CH

Queen of the Hill Publishing
P O Box 590
Lake Forest, IL 60045
www.queenofthehillpublishing.com

Publisher's Note: This is a work of fiction. Names, characters, places, and incidents are a product of the author's imagination. Locales and public names are sometimes used for atmospheric purposes. Any resemblance to actual people, living or dead, or to businesses, companies, events, institutions, or locales is completely coincidental.

Ordering Information:
Quantity sales. Special discounts are available on quantity purchases by corporations, associations, and others. For details, contact the "Special Sales Department" at the address above.

Cash Only: A Hoe Cartel/ TY NESHA. -- 1st ed.
ISBN 978-0-9973840-0-0

To my two beautiful daughters and family for their patience and support, my longtime friends, and new friends discovered during the writing and publishing of this work.

Cash-In!

"**W**here the fuck is my money?!" Meredith screamed, beating on the door. She was pissed and it appeared to be the only obstacle between her and Brains, her boss and lover. He owed her five grand and she wasn't going anywhere until she got it.

"I'd advise you to step away from the door bitch, 'fore I splatter them pretty little brains across that walkway."

His baritone voice vibrated through the walls, causing Meredith to become even more furious. See, Meredith was serious about her dough. If anyone should've known that, it was the man that had taught her everything she knew.

Brains never was much for introductions, but he was usually a man of his word and a hothead. So, he didn't usually forewarn you before he blew your brains out across the pavement that lay beneath your feet.

He stroked his thick, full beard seeming unfazed and continued counting the money spread across the glass coffee table. Slick—his young, fearless, fifteen-year-old, street soldier—

stood confidently nearby. He took his unofficial role as body-guard to a known hustler with street-cred serious. He was always holding his pistol in his dominant hand so he could drop into a ready position in a matter of moments.

"Look, I don't have time for this mess! I need my money now—not tomorrow, not in an hour. Now, muthafucka!" Meredith was done with his foolishness. She wasn't about to let Brains continue to taunt her.

She had been Brains' top hoe in the game. She'd helped him build his whole business from scratch. From the bottom on the corners, all the way up to the mansions. She went from bringing in change off the streets to rolling in anywhere from one to five grand in a day, depending on the services she provided.

Now she was ready to throw in the towel and give her daughter, Cashmere, a better life. She'd finally saved enough money to break free from the hoe stroll to do it.

"Now I told yo' high yella ass to go head on with all dat noise!" Brains yelled back. "I'm gone give you five seconds to re-think yo' strategy and get the fuck on, 'fore I light dis bitch up," he warned.

"You know what? I'm still leavin' yo' snake ass, with or without my money! So FUCK—"

BANG!

Before Meredith could even finish her sentence, the sharp, ear shattering blast of the bullet pierced right through the door.

It splintered the wood and crashed into her frontal lobe. Her body crumpled and fell limp like a rag doll across the stairway. Her blood poured furiously through her jet-black hair.

The crimson puddle quickly trickled its way toward ten-year-old Cashmere's small frame, frozen in fear and shock.

CHAPTER ONE

Cash: Smoke-n-Mirrors

My mama, Meredith, died when I was just ten years old. I'd stood there and watched the blood drain from her head, leaving me to clean up the mess she left behind. Mama was the first person I'd seen die, but she wouldn't be the last.

Meredith was a hustler and she'd taught me two valuable lessons in this game: never fuck for free and never fall in love. She'd broken both of those cardinal rules when she fell in love with a trick—then messed around and told Brains that she was done with the hoe game.

I guess you could say falling in love got my mama's head blown off, in broad daylight, leaving me without a mother, fatherless, and most likely to one day fill the shoes she'd left behind.

"In this game ladies, fuckin' is a business. Your pussy is the product. If you fall in love, you might as well be gettin' high off your own supply." I adjourned the meeting, leaving the girls enough time to let that concept simmer, so there would be no confusion when it came time for the money to be made. We have a major function coming up at a big venue in less than forty-eight hours. I already know these hoes can be all too quick to get shit twisted when those green, dead presidents start free-flowing.

Who am I? My government name is Cashmere Jones, though nearly everyone around here just calls me Cash. I'm a feisty chick but can't figure out if that's due to my Italian or my Black roots.

My presence seems to command attention everywhere I tread. I've been told I have a super thick, curvaceous, video-vixen body. The type that have daddies all dazed and confused, ready to risk it all for a chance to wrap these smooth, honey-toned thighs around their ears. It balances out nicely with my angelic face that leave mamas staring as they swallow sharp pangs of insecurity, licking their lips in appreciation. My sparkling green eyes contrast beautifully with my bronze skin and the freckles lightly sprinkled across the bridge of my nose.

But don't let the pretty face fool you. I have no problem takin' a nigga out, execution style, in the blink of an eye. I'm the triple threat that can be your wildest fantasy or your worst nightmare.

Overall, I'm a shrewd businesswoman with an analytical mind-set, goals, my associate's and bachelor's degrees, and a plan for vengeance. I intend to take what's mine.

Brains took me in under his wing and taught me everything I needed to know about LLE, Living Lavish Enterprises. We have over 25 factions throughout the US and Mexico that collaborate with the cartels. They are quickly multiplying and expanding. The enterprise only services the very best of the best. We serve upscale clientele such as athletes, doctors, lawyers, CEOs, and the like.

I quickly learned the ins and outs of the agency, leaving Brains impressed at how well I handled the business. Eventually, he promoted me to the top Madame position in the Los Angeles regional office. Our office just happens to be the headquarters of the leading enterprise in the industry.

Building my team wasn't easy. I had to strategically build my lineup from scratch, recruiting hoes from all walks of life. My goal was to finesse my team into the baddest, most beautiful, intelligent, no-nonsense hoes in the game.

I hauled in the best in the business: the street hoes, the expensive hoes, the reformed hoes, the new hoes, and even some of the overlooked hoes. In just two years, I'd gone from a five-hoe troop to a whole damn army of polished, upscale moneymakers.

Increasing LLE's revenue by over fifty million dollars in less than a year effectively made me the HBIC, or Head Bitch in Charge.

"Cash, I reviewed last week's summary of our financial reports and the enterprise's assets aren't adding up," Leslie announced from my office doorway just as I began to shut down and pack up for the night.

I motioned for her to come inside. "Have a seat," I advised. "Close the door behind you."

Leslie stood there contemplating the invite briefly. Her light blue eyes shimmered as they caught the late afternoon sun reflecting through the office windows. She glanced over at Jersey anxiously. Then her eyes fell back on mine, expressing that she would rather we speak in private.

"Look, bitch. I don't have all day to be toyin' around with your Playboy bunny–lookin' ass. Speak, hoe." I had no time for pleasantries. I was eager to get home to Brains to handle some serious business, as usual.

Jersey burst out in laughter. "That's what your uppity-ass get. Speak, hoe!" she snapped at Leslie in a gruff tone, mocking the failed attempt to exclude her from the conversation.

I made eye contact with Jersey giving her a slight smirk. Warning her silently to take it down a notch so we could finish and quickly get the hell up out of here.

Refusing to sit down, Leslie finally spoke up. "Fine. Apparently, there's been a mix up in the financial records. From the looks of it, Cash'Me'ers Boutique has generated three times more in revenue than the expected projections, which is nearly impossible."

"Nearly impossible based on *whose* expectations, Leslie?" I inquired sharply.

"Well the company's, of course," she scoffed sarcastically.

"Bitch, were you worried about the company's expectations when I pulled yo' pole-dancin' ass out the strip club? Or, should I pop one of them plastic-ass titties of yours to help trigger your memory?" I quipped. "Listen closely. I do not now, nor will I ever, fall under or within the expectations of any 'company.' I exceed expectations. So, the next time you decide to bring yo' ass up in my office after hours with some bullshit like this...oh you'd better come correct, Ms. Thing," I warned in a no-nonsense voice, staring directly into Leslie's eyes.

I closed my eyes briefly and inhaled a deep breath. I was trying to calm the bitterness I felt toward the young woman. I had to get back to some semblance of professionalism.

"Matter-of-fact, feel free to check the stats on the boutique and reevaluate the name. Every single penny that flows through that establishment has been masterminded by yours truly. You would do well to remember that the next time you try to set margins on what's possible, sweetie," I finished in a deceptively pleasant tone.

"Fuck outta here!" Jersey commanded, pointing toward the door.

Leslie flipped her blonde hair over her shoulder, shooting one last glance full of loathing in Jersey's direction and stormed out of the office like a scolded child.

LLE is one of my top priorities. I'm proud of the fact that we pose as the largest placement agency in all of Los Angeles. I was able to make this happen by strategically dividing my top girls into five diverse segments. The Accounting Firm, the Talent Agency, the Athletic Department, Party Promotion, and Housekeeping were always recruiting.

I'm in charge of keeping the operation running smoothly. I do it by cultivating a cunning smokescreen in order to maintain the perception of our establishment being as legit as possible.

Cash'Me'ers, on the other hand, is my baby. I'd assembled the boutique from the bottom up with my own blueprints, designs, merchandise, staff, and loyal customers. Cash'Me'ers earned well over projections for such a small business within the first few months of its grand opening, and the cash cow didn't stop there.

The boutique has quickly become one of the most popular, exclusive provisions off of Melrose. It's a magnet for the rich and famous, and even tourists, as one of the best dress shops in L.A. The steady earnings often left Brains stunned by the way that I handled my business.

Leslie, the snow bunny and former dancer, had been recruited from The Lux Gentlemen's Club, right on Hollywood

Boulevard. The bitch had a hell of a client list, too. She was your average blonde-haired, blue-eyed white chick that needed to feel superior in every aspect due to being fed with a silver spoon her entire life.

I'd converted her over into the team as the Certified Public Accountant of LLE. This, my friends, was the "proper" way of classifying her as a decoy in this organization. Frankly, the bitch was little more than the bookkeeper and rebellious, wayward daughter of the head police chief.

Leslie was designated to manage the accounting firm. She recruited college interns that serviced the professors, rich college kids, and their daddies. The interns were bringing in anywhere from twenty to twenty-five stacks each over the course of just a few days.

"Yo, I don't like that trashy bitch, son," Jersey ranted as she pulled her reddish-brown hair back into a bun, highlighting her big, brown eyes and deeply-pierced dimples.

"She wants your spot, Cash, na' mean? That bitch buggin'. She know good and well she be frontin', rentin' all that knock-off shit. She don't own none of that shit. Not even them fake-ass titties she be flauntin'."

"Them thangs be mad sexy though," I joked with a giggle.

"Hell yeah. Sittin' up all perky and shit. Like two juicy-ass melons ready to hydrate all them thirsty-ass college boys."

We shared a good laugh. Jersey has no filter. She wasn't afraid to do or say shit, and that's exactly how I liked it.

Some people choose the game. For others, the game chooses them. Jersey and I were both chosen to play this game. We were given only one check box, already auto-filled with a "yes".

Although Jersey was born in the Caribbean she'd been raised in Brooklyn. She was always leaving folks amazed by her exquisite beauty and style. They always fell in love with her gutter, street-savvy, New York charisma.

Jersey and I met a few years back when I was out in Brooklyn on a run for Brains. She just so happened to roll up in the middle of an altercation. I nearly got jumped by some rough hood bitches while attempting to collect one of Brains' unpaid debts.

Jersey, only fifteen years old at the time, stepped in and fought alongside me like we were the coolest of family members. We whooped ass that day. From then on, we were inseparable.

Now, with all my current responsibilities and obligations, I'm too damn busy to fight. I'd rather cock and load my burner than risk messing up my moneymaker.

Each of my LLE ladies has developed a decoy guise, along with a team that they are responsible for educating, guiding, and keeping in line. Their jobs are really quite simple. Perform your duties and collect your riches in full. No shorts and no freebies.

After collecting their payments, the girls report in to Leslie. Leslie kéeps the books in order, pays the girls, and manages some of the enterprise's other assets.

"Yo, it's 8:30. I got a nine o'clock on Sunset Boulevard. I'll hit you up tomorrow, Cash," Jersey tossed over her shoulder, rushing out.

I barely heard a word that had come out of her mouth, anyway. After receiving a text from Brains, my attention shifted instantly.

Brains: *"Meet me at the spot in 1 hr."*

Me: *"Bet."*

I had just enough time to shower in my newly remodeled office space before meeting him. After months of complaining about not having enough space, Brains had finally granted me the addition, with my own personal bathroom and relaxing sitting area, as a birthday gift. Whatever alterations he made, regardless of which area in his life, Brains made sure that it was always an upgrade to bigger and better.

Walking into my private room after a full day of work made me appreciate any down time I could get. Sighing with contentment, I realized how proud I was of the accomplishments I'd made. The money continuously rolled in, twenty-four hours a day. After investing in my boutique and paying the girls and Brains, I still had more than enough money to live, worry-free.

Meredith would be proud, I thought to myself. Thinking about Mama never made me sad. She'd always said, "*In this world, ain't no room for tears. You get no respect being weak, let alone a woman. You got to earn your respect and take what's yours in the process.*" She would always finish it up by saying, "*Cash, the world is yours, baby!*"

All bullshit aside, the day she was murdered, I cried. I cried a river. Mama would've frowned on that, but I didn't care.

That was the day I learned that in this lonely world you can't trust nobody to have your back, and you'd better watch the company you keep.

Brains had no fucking idea that I was with Mama when he blew a hole in her head. I collected my things along with Mama's special bag and jetted the fuck out of the hallway before I was next.

Brains found me next door in the two-story home he and Mama shared, pretending to be fast asleep.

"*Cashmere, wake up,*" *he said, his tone gravelly. His massive body stood next to my bed. His eyes peered closely at me.*

I rubbed my eyes as if my sleep had been disturbed and I was disoriented. "*Brains, what's wrong?*" *I asked, pretending to be oblivious.*

"*Ya mama done got herself shot. She dead, babygirl. She gone!*

My musings were interrupted as I felt a tear trickle down my cheek. Baffled, I wiped the wetness away gently. This was the first time I'd shed one since the night of the murder. Hell, I didn't even cry at Mama's funeral.

I just sat there numb, strategizing all the different ways to get that nigga, Brains, six feet under. Watching him stand over Mama's cocaine-white casket, with fake tears and a red rose, made my stomach churn. Before the casket closed, I would scoop the rose off of Mama's body to preserve it for the day I'd seek my retribution.

It was imperative that I learn as much as I could about the organization. So, for eleven years I've plotted my way to the top. Getting there left me with fewer things to check off my to-do list. Now my focus was squarely on conspiring to take over the enterprise. I planned to do that by getting clout by touching "the untouchables."

In any business, respect is never given. You've got to earn it. Being a woman in this game, you have to learn how to take it. That's just what I intend to do.

Taking out the orchestrator of the enterprise would surely prove to be difficult, but there's nothing more challenging than pretending to adore the muthafucka that took my mama's last breath!

Checklist:

Earn Brains' trust.

Move up the ladder of the cartel.

Kill Brains.

CASH OUT!

CHAPTER TWO
Jersey: A Hoe Is a Hoe

Rihanna's "Bitch Betta Have My Money" blasted from my speakers, nearly blowing them out. I banged that joint loud as hell as my cream-colored Benz pulled up to the hotel.

The valet greeted me before I could even take my foot off the brake. These muthafuckas knew me all too well. The cute Latino *papi* rushed over to open my door, greeting me with a smile and extending his hand.

"Well, aren't you quite the gentleman today," I said with a giggle. I could see his dick print rising through his pants as he admired my strong, bronze legs. I gave him a sneak peak of my smooth, perfectly-waxed pussy as I stepped out of the car.

I stood up, pulling down my white Phillip Lim miniskirt, and licked my lips just for the hell of it. I leaned in toward the handsome fella, allowing my perky tits to distract him as I groped his dick.

"You would be a good fuck, but..." I leaned in closer and licked his earlobe softly before continuing my statement. "You can't afford me. Now, would you kindly park my shit, before I charge your ass double for the show?"

The man shot me a look of disgust before moving to do what I'd said, thinking twice before saying something he'd later regret.

For a Tuesday night, WeHo and the strip was rocking. I glanced over at the underrated corner hoes in revulsion. I watched as they leaned their thirsty asses inside the rides that stopped at the lights.

Scrutinizing them left me with a bad taste in my mouth. I thought to myself, if they only knew the power those worn-out pussies contained. They'd be right here walking into the Pink Palace, demanding nothing but the finest, instead of standing out there on the front lines.

I know y'all probably thinking, *look at this "upscale hoe" judging the "low-class hoes."* Any way you look at it, a hoe is a hoe, right? Nah, wrong!

It's all sorts of hoes in this game. There's the ones that fuck simply because they long to feel wanted, the ones that are out here merely fuckin' for a nut, and the ones on the street corners getting fucked and discarded within moments—for pennies—to support their addictions or equally motivating factors. Then you got my clique, the brothel bitches of LLE. In this enterprise, fuckin' is just the cherry on top.

You'd be surprised to learn the level of notoriety of some of the clients walking through our doors. We get paid mad *guap* just to accompany these men to an event. Or, sometimes, just to hold a conversation with them. On a bad day, we still get paid five stacks to pretend like two minutes of quick thrusting is two hours of pure ecstasy.

On top of that, the nigga Brains don't see a penny of my money, aside from what I pay for the cover-up. Shit, you might as well say we break even in that department, because we give his ass a legit purpose as well.

See, that's what I like about Cash: everything is business with her. She managed to convince Brains to see us as a valuable commodity in this enterprise. He'll eventually view us as invaluable business partners once the pussy business places him in the company of the right individuals at just the right time. That'll create a shitload of opportunities for his drug enterprise to thrive. It'll also help Brains position himself as the head of the most respected, high-end, cartel-connected drug enterprise in Los Angeles and us as the highest paid and protected hoes in the business. If you ask me, Cash is pimpin' him and he ain't even know it.

This enterprise is my only means of a "legit" job in L.A., being that I don't have my papers and all. I was ten years old, kicking and screaming, when I was trafficked out of Honduras. My junkie-ass mother was a gutter bitch that would sell her own mama if she could. Since she couldn't do that, she sold me instead.

"Azalea? This is Mister Garcia. He thinks you are very beautiful," my mother announced, like it was a fucking award ceremony, or some shit.

I'd looked over his clean-shaven face, stocky build, and light skin, knowing he was way out of his weight class and out of line. "Thank you, Mister Garcia," I spoke softly, extending my hand. I was hoping this uncomfortable scene ended quickly. "It was very nice meeting you," I said. Before I could push past the big man and excuse myself, my mother blocked my path, continuing her ceremonial speech.

"Mister Garcia give me good monies for your company. So, I need you to be very nice and cooperative, Lea!"

I was far from stupid. I knew exactly what this was. I tried to flee by running toward the opposite end of the room, only to be apprehended by Mister Garcia's accomplice.

Turned out, this would be the last day that I would see my hometown. I turned my head to stare into her eyes and face the disgrace of a woman and mother as a cascade of tears ran down my cheeks.

"It'll be just fine, Azalea. They take good care of you. Just listen to Mister Garcia and don't make any troubles." Her words faded out quickly, and so did Azalea.

The elevator pinged, signaling my arrival onto the penthouse floor of The Beverly Hills Hotel. I quickly fixed my face, freshened up my lipstick, and smoothed out my hair before exiting the elevator.

Back to the basics, I thought, entering the suite of my number one client, NBA Commissioner Marc Winston. I let myself in and closed the door silently behind me. I was careful not to interrupt Marc, who was obviously on a heated business call. I slipped into the bathroom and primed myself for the evening.

When I met with Marc I always had to give myself the "pep talk." Marc and I spent a lot of time together, much more than what was customary for my other clients. In fact, I had to blow off the others when he came calling, and let's just say...this fella here was well worth it!

I examined myself in the bathroom mirror and exhaled deeply before mumbling through my "night with Marc" speech. "Look bish. This is business, a hustle, and an on-goin' fantasy. You bet not fall nowhere, but on that man's enormous dick. Fallin' in love is a no-no! This is none other than a high-payin' porn. And you, my dear, have the starrin' role!"

CHAPTER THREE
Brains: Hollywood Bliss

"I'm not even gone think twice 'bout slicin' yo' throat if all my money ain't here. I'm the wrong muthafucka to be fuckin' with," I calmly announced, slowly closing the oversized briefcase. I'm serious about my business. After partnering up with one of the Mexican cartels, I was manufacturing enough product and building up franchises to dominate the industry. Today, I was meeting with my connect, Javier Mendoza.

I cautiously examined the other briefcase filled with Hollywood Bliss, the fastest growing substance in the cartel at the moment. "Look, this shit is dangerous if it's not separated carefully," I explained. Javier wore a bizarre look on his face, which made me a little uneasy myself, but I was ready for whatever. I blew a gust of cigar smoke in the air. "Now, make sure you check the shit. Make sure it's legit. 'Cause I don't want no issues later. You feel me?"

Javier was known for being shady as hell. So, I wanted to ensure there was no bullshit from his ass. He cut the package down the middle before sticking his finger in, then snorted a small portion into his nostril. "Whooo...shit," he sniffed and shook his head, confirming what I already knew. "Now, that shit is some good shit, my man!"

I nodded at Slick to bring in the rest of the product. Three briefcases later, Javier decides to question the final bulk of the packages.

"Nah, motherfucker. This shit ain't the same as the others," Javier declared, pinching his chin.

Slick chuckled.

"Mah muthafuckin nigga!" I hollered. "Now, didn't I call this shit, Slick?"

Since we were linked to the cartels, I'd already gotten the low-down on Javier and his bullshit antics. I'd hoped the fool had sounder judgement. He obviously didn't, if he thought he was going to insult my intelligence. I stared at Mr. Javier Mendoza with hostile, narrowed eyes. My jaw began to throb.

Without taking my eyes off him, I tilted my head to the side, giving him a crooked smirk. "You know somethin'? Maybe you right," I told him, as if complying with his demand. "Slick, run me that last package in the back for Mr. Javier and his lovely entourage," I called over my shoulder, maintaining eye contact with the grimy Hispanic.

Javier cocked his gun, and his sidekick followed suit, indirectly warning me not to try anything crazy.

"You might wanna think twice, 'fore you raise that heat over here, homie," Slick warned, as he moved toward the storage area. He pulled back the curtains, revealing the beautiful, older Hispanic woman tied to the chair, tears rolling down her face.

"What the fuck, man!" Javier yelled, viciously. "Chu motherfuckers!"

Javier hadn't expected to see his mother here at tonight's meeting. I was always two steps ahead, pulling the dirtiest tricks out my sleeves right when I knew they would matter the most.

I slowly removed the tape from her mouth, as she sat bound to the chair with rope. The tape had already started turning her pretty brown ankles and wrists a bright pink.

"Hello, pretty lady," I said in a sensual tone, stroking the woman's cheek.

She immediately started to plead for her life. "Please, just let me go. I won't make trouble. Please! Javier, tell the man you won't make trouble. Please...he has your sister, Natalia! You have to make nice with the man!"

The woman was nothing but a distraction to throw Javier off his square. Slick followed along with the plan, knowing that the woman would pose no threat to our current disposition.

Javier's mother's eyes widened suddenly like she'd just seen a ghost. Slick had managed to silently maneuver himself over to the opposite side of the room. He now held two revolvers aimed directly at both Javier and his sidekick's craniums, causing them to carefully drop their weapons.

"Now, how 'bout you check the packages one more time. I'm sure you might change yo' mind," I chuckled.

Javier eyed me and said, "Man, this shit is fucked up. And you bring *mi madre* into this shit, man?" he fumed.

"You know Javier, we could've been great partners. But you don't seem to know how to be a business man without pullin' these snake-ass moves." I walked up on him, looking him square in his eyes. "Now, we can handle this shit like men. Or, we can handle this shit like some fuckin' goons. Yo' choice."

Suddenly Javier lunges for my piece, stuffed down the front of my pants, just as I calculated he'd do. I quickly snatched the machete out of my side sheath, stabbing him straight in the gut. Twisting and turning the broad, heavy knife, I watched his blood pour out of the wound, dark and heavy, leaving his body limp.

His mother began to whimper. I grabbed my piece and shot that bitch dead in the face.

"What the *fuck*, man?" Slick panicked.

"Clean this shit up," I ordered, exiting the room. I didn't linger around to babysit those fools either. I had shit to do. Slick was more than capable of handling business and cleaning up the mess, including finishing off Javier's right-hand man.

I was definitely sending a message. I was well aware of who I'd just murdered. Although Javier was notorious in the game, so the fuck am I. I'll worry about the aftereffects and fallout later.

All I could think about on the way home was Cash. When I made her responsible for the hoes, I never imagined she would pull shit off the way she has. That girl never fails to get the job done. That shit made my dick hard, every time.

She reminded me so much of her mama. Although I raised her, I sure as hell ain't never been her daddy. I made that clear from Day One.

Meredith was a hardhead bitch. Although she was also a smart woman with a lot of class. She'd messed up by trying to make it her business to question my every move, trying to dictate policies around my organization.

Now, don't get me wrong, she knew her shit. However, Meredith somehow managed to forget her place and I just couldn't have that shit. She was my bottom bitch, my main bitch, and my classy bitch. Somewhere along the way, she forgot...she was *my* bitch!

"Look, Brains, shit ain't the same no more, and..." I tried to interrupt, putting my hand up to silence her. She had the audacity to keep talking. "I'm ready to make some different moves. You know...expand and shit!"

I yoked her ass up, quicker than the words had left her pretty little lips. I never once had to put my hands on Meredith, but she was becoming a disrespectful-ass hoe!

"Look, bitch. Shit don't expand until I say it's time to expand. I made you, hoe, and I have no problem breakin' yo' ass."

Meredith stared back in my face, never once showing any sign of fear. As I stared back into her hazel eyes, I noticed they had lost the fire in them. The fire that had once burned between her and I was long gone. I slowly released my grip from her neck. "Damn, baby. See what you done made me do? I..."

SLAP!

This bitch lost her mind and smacked me in my face!

"Now, you listen here, Brian. There ain't a nigga on the streets of L.A. that can take credit for the bitch that stands before you today!" she said between clenched teeth, calling me by my government name.

It took everything inside of me not to fuck her ass up, right then and there. Hell, if her daddy wasn't "the man" of the city at the time, I would've. But the bitch was right.

Meredith was self-made. Not even her shady-ass pops could take credit for that. I actually rocked with that shit, 'cause the bitch never needed me for a damn thing. I loved that about her.

I love that about her fine-ass daughter, Cash, too.

I pulled up at the house, noticing Cash had beat me home as usual. I glanced up at my reflection in the rearview mirror. I tightened my eyes and licked my lips. I was quite pleased with the person I saw staring back.

I thought to myself, *for a forty-five-year-old, I sholl am a sexy nigga.* My waves and goatee stay shaped up, just as full as they were when I was in my early twenties.

"I get betta by the second, baby!" I chanted, hopping out my ride. When I entered the crib, slow music was playing softly. The vibe was very calming.

"Cash! Baby, where you at?" I called out. At that very moment, I raised my eyes to see her standing at the top of the staircase. She was a vision of beauty, looking something like that actress, Stacy Dash, in the face and a fucking stallion from her neck down.

I couldn't help being mesmerized. Not just by her small waist and thick ass, but even more so by how much Cash had blossomed from that young girl into a grown woman.

She pressed her lips together in a sexy pout as she leaned over the railing. Her body was oiled up and her six inch heels made my dick throb.

"So, you just gone stand there, daddy? Or, you gone come get this pussy?"

CHAPTER FOUR

Leslie: Underestimated

Cashmere really has some nerve—speaking to me like I'm scum at the bottom of her shoe. To top it off, she lets that bitch, Jersey, have way too much say-so. I really underestimated that girl. I still don't believe the boutique racked up all that legal money in such a short time. And, I'm going to get to the bottom of it, sooner rather than later.

I know what you're thinking. I'm jealous of Cashmere, right? Fuck yes. I really do envy that bitch! However, coming soon, I plan to have everything she has—including that hot-ass boss of ours, Brian. That bitch doesn't even know what to do with a man like him.

Ring...

"Living Lavish Enterprises, this is Leslie speaking..." I answered the telephone on the first ring, already having a pretty good idea of who would be on the other end.

"Leslie, you missed dinner again last night. Now, you promised you wouldn't..."

I quickly interrupted my annoying mother before my head could explode. "Yes, Mother. I know, and I sincerely apologize," I interjected lamely, rolling my eyes. "This job entails much more than average and I need to be on my toes, if I want this promotion," I lied.

My mother sighed deeply into the phone.

Before she could give me a forty-five-minute lecture, I continued. "How about, first thing Friday morning? I'll take you out for breakfast. We can do some shopping and have a little 'girl talk.'"

Mother sighed again but this time it was a sigh of relief. I could picture her sitting at the dining room table, putting together one of her five-thousand piece puzzles and sipping her favorite Hazelnut coffee.

"I'll hold you to that, honey. Make sure you call your father. He's been worried sick about his princess."

I rolled my eyes again before responding. "Yes, Mother. I will get to that very soon. I have another call," I lied, rushing her off the phone. "I love you...bye!" I quickly pressed the button on the switch hook, releasing her call.

Still holding the receiver, I started to call my dad. I had only pressed the first four numbers before deciding against it. I slammed the telephone down into its cradle.

Sitting at my desk, I sipped from my wine glass and began to reflect. Since I'd begun working in the enterprise, time seemed to quickly fly by. It's been just over a year and while I hate to admit it—Cashmere was right. My expectations could never envision bringing in the type of money that I do.

Overall, my job is a piece of cake. It's a mixture of customer service and fantasy fulfillment. What's not to love about that? On top of that, I don't have to ask my father for shit. He's pissed that he can no longer use his credit cards as a form of control over me. I have my own fucking black card now and Father despises that.

I decided to wrap it up for the night and began to collect my things. I couldn't help gritting my teeth when I saw Cashmere's arrogant ass brush past my office. "Snooty bitch," I mumbled under my breath. The nerve of her, to think she's so much fucking better than me. That bitch is going to slip up. And when she does, I'm going to step in. If she doesn't, I just may have to pull the rug right out from underneath her, my damn self. That'll teach her ass a lesson, for underestimating me.

"You called for housekeeping?" A soft, Latina voice interrupted my thoughts of destruction.

"I sure did. Come on in, Natalia," I answered, pulling up the last two requests of the evening. Natalia's eyes lit up as she quickly skimmed the client list. I could see the dollar signs in her eyes before she picked up her phone. Natalia rapidly fired off a series of text messages, before preparing to exit my office.

"Natalia, aren't you forgetting something?" I asked quizzically, with a tilt of my head.

She chuckled, reaching into her purse. "No, Miss Leslie. I no forget your monies," she replied in her thick accent, pulling out an envelope full of hundreds and placing it on my desk.

I counted the money before shooing her on her way. She grumbled a few words at me, in Spanish, before hastily exiting my office.

Just as I got ready to head out, the telephone rang, again. With a deep sigh of resignation, I answered. "Hello, Father."

CHAPTER FIVE

Cash: Twisted

I stared down at his sexy ass. At first, he was standing at the bottom of the staircase, staring up at me. With every step he took toward me, I was exposed to some form of masculine beauty that this man wore gracefully on his frame.

The man is fine as fuck. I could definitely see what Mama saw in his conniving ass. Standing 6'2" and 220 pounds, he sported big, rock-solid muscles and the most beautiful, smooth, caramel skin you'd ever want to see. His thick goatee was complimented by the sexiest mustache sitting on top of his full lips. It gave him an aura of seriousness and mystique. And it made me moist as I imagined my pussy juices all over it.

I'd made it home, just in time, to set the scene for his arrival. I lit the candles and began playing my slow jams playlist softly in the background. Then, I stepped back and admired my handiwork.

The flames from the flickering candles reflecting in my eyes seemed to represent the fire I had burning inside of me. I was full of rage and resentment. Don't get me wrong, I'd definitely grown to love him. How could I *not* love this man? But my love for him wouldn't stand in the way of the mission at hand, which was strictly inevitable.

"Daddy, I've got something special for you," I teased, undoing the silk ties and allowing my Olivia von Halle lace robe to fall to the floor, away from my golden body. "I'm sure you've had a long day. So I want you to sit back and relax while I give you a show."

"Dance for You" by *Beyoncé* resounded from the speakers as I performed one hell of a routine. I added the stripper pole in the middle of the room to my performance. I slid down the pole seductively, revealing my pierced clit with every twist and turn. He licked his lips, groping his rock-hard dick.

"You know daddy love you, right?" He assured me as he watched me gyrate and wave my arms and hips through the air, lip-syncing the words to the song.

I nodded my head, acknowledging what he'd just professed to me. "Is that right, daddy?" I asked playfully as I moved closer and mounted him.

"Fuck, yeeaaah," he hissed through clenched teeth. He gripped my body, guiding his hard dick into my dripping wet opening. I rotated my hips in a swivel, every which way, and watched his light-brown eyes roll into the back of his head. The way he filled me up was enough to send me over the edge, screaming for mercy.

"Damn, Cash." He groped my body, pleasuring me with the slightest touch, as he met my thrusts. "This pussy is so fuckin' good, girl," he whispered, as he squeezed and stroked my hips and ass.

I answered him with moans while rocking my body.

"Oh shit," he groaned. "That's it, bitch...fuck me!"

Him slapping my ass and calling me a bitch turned me on even more. I started fucking the shit out of his ass, even harder, as sweat poured down our bodies.

He put his fingers inside my mouth. I sucked on them erotically, until I began to shake uncontrollably.

"That's right, baby. Get that shit. Let that pussy cum all over this dick," he commanded, holding me tighter, matching my force.

"Fuck, baby. That's it, right there. Don't stop, baby." He let out a loud, guttural moan, letting me know his ejaculation was close.

On cue, I released all my own sweet juices, echoing his warning cry with my own loud, satisfied moan. I continued to thrust for a moment, riding the euphoric waves of the intense climax in slow motion. Then I quickly hopped off before he could release and wrapped my lips around his swollen, throbbing dick saturated with my essence.

I attempted to suck every single drop out of him while he pleaded, weakly.

"Wait...wait...wait..."

Ignoring his pleas, I continued my mission, leaving him drained.

"Now, *that's* how you welcome yo' man home, baby!" Satisfied, he gave a lazy chuckle, right before passing out.

The ringing phone woke me up out of my sleep. You would think whoever was calling would've gotten the hint the first three times I ignored their asses.

"This better be important, Ev," I answered, with a growl, wiping the drool off my mouth.

"Cash, I need your help! Carlos did it again. I... I..." She began crying hysterically.

Whatever had gone down, I knew it had to be major, because Evelyn never cried. She was easily one of the most resilient chicks I'd ever met, aside from Jersey and Vic. She was also very humble and optimistic, always looking on the brighter side to a glass half-full and shit.

"Where you at, girl? Calm down. I'm on my way!"

On my way to Evelyn's house I couldn't help thinking the worst. When she'd said Carlos' name, I thought for sure that he had gone upside her head again.

Evelyn is another one of my best girls in the enterprise. We met two years ago at the boutique. Her beauty and thick Spanish accent caught my attention instantly.

"Jasmine, you straight trippin', girl! Look, all you gotta do is pin ya hair up, like this..."

I stood back and watched her try to convince her slightly overweight friend that she could rock whatever she wanted, as she pulled a variety of pieces from the racks. Her technique was amazing. I knew exactly where she would fit in at LLE.

"You ladies see something you like?" I'd asked, simultaneously scoping Evelyn out from head to toe.

Just looking at her, she appeared to be Puerto Rican, maybe, mixed with a little Black. She was a real pretty chick with a nice little shape. Her ass wasn't as big as mine, but it was still a fatty.

"Well, actually..." she began, curving her lips into a pleasant smile.

I couldn't help but notice how beautiful she was, aside from all of the make-up caked onto her face, attempting to hide an obvious black eye. She read the concern in my eyes and quickly turned away. Then she passed me a few garments.

"Can my friend try these on?" she asked.

"Good choices," I said, commending her fashion sense. "Michelle, can you show this young lady to the dressing room, please?" I asked one of the boutique associates.

"You are a very beautiful girl. If you don't mind me asking, what do you do?" I asked, under the guise of making small talk, yet wasting no time getting down to business.

Still not willing to look directly at me again, she formed a pretty smile. "I model and dance," she replied.

"You a stripper?" I pointedly asked.

She chuckled. "Nah, girl. But if I had a little more up here, I would definitely shake this ass and slide down somebody's pole," she guaranteed, gripping her B-cups.

I stared at her like she'd lost her damn mind, then chuckled and shook my head. The question I asked myself was, "What the hell is wrong with these hoes?"

We shared a laugh and chatted another moment or two. It took me all of five minutes to recruit Evelyn onto my team.

It only took her six months to prove herself. She simultaneously worked her way into my heart and earned her spot as my top bitch in the modeling and dancing area of LLE.

If it wasn't for her love and devotion to that bum-ass nigga, Carlos, I would've silenced his ass a long time ago. He really seemed to think he was superior to women; his coward ass had no respect.

I finally pulled up to Evelyn's crib and before I could even turn off Ms. Porsche, my pet name for my diva of a car, I recognize Evelyn's silhouette. She was pacing across her front room as my headlights beamed into her windows.

I hopped out of my car and darted through the slightly cracked front door. "Yo, Ev!" I called out.

When she didn't answer, I knew something had to be wrong. She seemed like she was really out of it, in shock maybe. It was almost like she was in a trance. Her hair was pulled back into a messy bun and her shirt was ripped.

When she finally turned to face me, I noticed her clothing was drenched in blood. "What the *fuck*, Evelyn?" I screamed, running toward her to make sure she was okay.

She fell into my arms, crying and blubbering some shit in Spanish.

"Bitch, speak English!" I hissed at her, losing my cool.

She stared at me, broken, eyes overflowing with tears. "I kill him, Cash! I kill him!"

CHAPTER SIX

Slick: Straight Disrespectful

"**D**on't that muthafucka know he just started a fuckin' war, Slick?" Larry worried, pacing back and forth.

"Yep," I replied calmly, taking a toke from the blunt. Larry was getting on my nerves with all this whining, like a little-ass bitch. "Nigga, if you don't sit yo' pussy ass down somewhere, you gone be joining Javier and his homie," I warned, exhaling thick smoke out into the room.

That nigga stopped dead in his tracks. "Slick, that's some fucked-up shit, bruh!"

For the life of me, I couldn't understand why the fuck Brains had these clowns on his squad. Shit, I don't agree with the way he handled that shit either, but what's done is done. If them fools want to rumble, they just better bring the heat.

All bullshit aside, the longer I stay on Brains' team, the more I despise him. He's becoming more of a monster by the minute. The money is good. Brains just ain't wrapped too tight.

Javier, on the other hand, had to pay for crossing the establishment. I knew the only way he would give us what we needed, without a brawl, was to bring in his sweet, sexy-ass mama. There was really no better way to use someone as bait, especially when you got the bait already on your team.

I had Claudia's head gone, the way I tried to fuck the lining out her pussy over these last few months. Finding out how much she despised her son, Javier, was just the icing on the cake. She knew exactly what she was getting her snake-of-a-son into. She believed he deserved every portion of what was to come. Killing her wasn't in the plan, but that nigga Brains obviously did what the fuck he wanted to.

"Aye, I got a few rounds to make. Go home and pull ya self together. Quit all that bitch ass whining," I advised, flicking my bud roach across the room.

Larry shot me a glance and nodded, but something in his face didn't seem right. I guess that's something I'll have to deal with at a later time. Right now I have other shit to tend to.

I pulled up in front of Brains' crib just in time to see Cash's fine ass walking—or should I say running—out the door. She was beautiful, even in sweat pants and a damn tank top. I could tell she ain't have on no panties by the way her ass jiggled. Made me want to stop her and fuck the shit out of her, right there in the damn driveway. I waited until she pulled off, then entered the crib using my spare key.

"Fuck you been?" Brains asked. He was in the cut, sitting in the dark. He took a long pull from his cigar, exposing a smug grin on his face.

"The fuck you smilin' at, nigga?" I asked sharply, flicking on the light. "That shit you did today was foul as fuck, man! Don't you know what you just sta—"

He interrupted my rant. "You scared now, nigga?"

I just glared at his bitch ass through narrowed eyes. My lip began to twitch. I slowly licked my lips and rubbed my hands together. "Nigga, I'm not even gone entertain that shit with a answer. But the next time you decide to switch some shit up..."

He put his hand up, with the intent to silence me.

"Fuck I look like? One of ya runners? Or, one of ya bitches? Nah, muthafucka. You don't silence me, my nigga!" Brains knew how I was when it came to questioning my gangsta, especially when it came to these streets.

"Nigga, sit yo' ass down and relax. Fuck you getting all worked up for?" Brains chuckled, trying to ease some of the tension out the room and lighten up the atmosphere.

Back in the day, he was the nigga behind the scenes orchestrating shit. Today he's regulating the inner-city drug trade, flooding the streets and the opposition with a purer product, Hollywood Bliss, at a better price. Now it seems like he's becoming a cold and heartless monster. I knew that was just another spoonful of bullshit he was feeding to the world, though.

I sat on the couch massaging my chin. "So, what's the next step, *Brainssss?*" I asked sarcastically.

"Why you trippin', man?" he asked, as he took out a sample of the Bliss and prepared to snort that bullshit up his nose.

I wanted to slap fire from his dumb, inconsiderate ass. He must've read my mind, 'cause he started rambling about some shit I really didn't give two fucks about. For now, I pushed that shit to the back of my mind.

"Look man, you really need to be snortin' up a plan, before shit get out of hand. I need a fuckin' drink." I got up to leave but that nigga grabbed my arm to stop me. I snatched away, not even bothering to look back.

His pussy ass ain't want to see me and he knew it. This nigga knows how I get down. He's known from Day One, when I saved his ass fifteen years ago. I hopped in my ride, blasting Kendrick Lamar, and lit up another blunt. I started thinking about how the fuck I ended up working for this clown...

The nigga was at the neighborhood gas station, right across from where I was posted, pumping some gas. He was hollerin' at some hoes, not even payin' attention to his surroundings.

I remember admiring his clean, red, old-school ride. I was just chillin' out front, imagining myself in a shiny stunna, just like his. All of a sudden, in the cars reflection, I see some niggas runnin' up on him. His slow ass ain't even see 'em coming. When he turned around, I recognized him from around the way.

He would see me hanging around the neighborhood and toss a few dollars my way from time to time. I'd just nod and put that shit in my pocket, nonchalantly. So this night, I felt like I owed it to him to help his clueless ass out of this jam.

I hopped off the stoop and rushed them niggas, airing they asses out one-by-one. The last one was crawling across the pavement. So, I took it upon myself to finish the job and shot his ass in the back of the head. His body went limp as his splattered blood decorated my apparel. That nigga, Brains, just stood there, all shook up and shit, barely able to move.

"They was 'bout to leave yo' ass leakin', my nigga," I assured him, before pulling my hood over my dreads and walking off.

Two weeks later, he approached me. "Aye, little homie, let me holla at you!"

I walked up to that shiny bitch, admiring it even more in the daylight. It was a 1973 Chevelle SS, cranberry red with two white racing stripes on the hood, a white vinyl top, white leather bench seat interior, and a 454 engine.

"What's good?" I nodded.

He chuckled. "I like ya style, little man."

I mugged his ass like he was crazy. "Little man? Nigga, I'm just as big as yo' ass. My name Slick, homie," I informed him.

"Slick, huh? Where ya mama at?"

"Mama dead. Daddy dead," I responded nonchalantly, still eying his ride.

"You like this shit, Slick?" he asked, patting the frame of the whip.

I just nodded at him. "Yeah, shit tight."

He hopped out the ride. "You know how to drive?"

"Yep," I replied.

He tossed me the keys. "It's yours!"

Just like that, I was on that nigga team. So for that nigga to question my gangsta...that shit there was straight disrespectful!

CHAPTER SEVEN

Evelyn: One-Way Trip to Safety

I opened my eyes and could've sworn the room was spinning. I was lying belly up, still unable to wrap my head around the previous night's events.

My wet hair felt like heavy vines against my face as I struggled to get out of bed. My body decided against me getting up, rewarding me with light-headedness instead for my haste.

I might have thought I was in a bad dream, were it not for the large knot embedded in my forehead. I was in so much pain I didn't know which was worse, the excruciating headache or the way my heart beat erratically against my chest, like it was being held captive inside of my severely beaten body.

"You finally decided to wake your red ass up, huh?" Cash sat across from me, leaning back in the chair.

I looked around the unfamiliar room in confusion. "Where are we?" Hearing myself speak aloud startled me, 'cause I didn't sound like myself one bit.

"Safe, is where you are now, Ev," Cash answered, before walking toward the bed. "That fool did a number on you this time," she said, blotting the warm towel over my bruises.

I turned away from her, trying to hold back the tears.

"Nah, bitch. Let them fuckers fall onto your face. So you can bury them right next to that bastard's body!"

My heart dropped. I could feel a lump forming in my throat. "I killed him, Cash..."

"No, I did."

I thought I heard her say she killed Carlos, but that was just my mind playing tricks on me. "Cash, what did you say? I didn't hear you correctly."

Cash put the towel down and backed away from the bed. "Oh, you heard what the fuck I said. *I killed him*!"

I felt like the room was closing in on me. My breathing grew heavy. I felt like the oxygen evaporated from the room. I started gasping for air.

"You...killed...him? That...that's impossible, Cash. I killed him! I saw him lying there, covered in blood. He wasn't moving!" I screeched, rapidly shaking my head in confusion, as if I could shake the vision from my mind.

Cash remained calm, although I could see a hint of hurt in her majestic, green eyes. She stood over me with her arms folded, eyes cold. It was like she really didn't even give a shit about what the fuck had just happened.

I squinted my eyes and began searching around the room with purpose. Eyes landing on what I was looking for, I quickly grabbed for my phone. She snatched it out of my trembling hand.

"What the fuck you think you doing?" she asked, scowling at me like I was next in line.

"Calm down, Cash! We have to call my papa. He can fix this. He will make it better," I assured her.

She stared at me like I had lost my mind. "I don't need your damn pappy to fix this shit, girl. I..." Cash stepped away from the bed, planting her hands on her wide hips. She took a deep breath.

"Look, Evelyn. I have a few of your girls on their way here to look after you for a few days," she explained in a calmer tone. "You have to take some time off, and I'm not taking 'no' for an answer. Natalia and her crew are at your place cleaning up. You'll be staying here until we find you someplace else to stay. As for right now, your ass is under my strict advisement to rest up."

I opened my mouth to protest, but she placed her finger over my lips.

"Shhh, babygirl, that sick fucker was going to take your life sooner rather than later. I just couldn't have that. You knocked his ass out, but you didn't kill him," she confessed, shaking her head. "Just be grateful you didn't do that shit. You're not built for the shit that haunts you after a murder, ma."

The tears trickled down my face as I lay helpless in bed. I knew what Cash was saying was true. Just knowing that she had saved me from a no-win situation made me respect her ten times more.

Although my father was the top defense attorney in his firm, I knew that me being labeled a murderer would crush him deeply and tarnish his reputation, even if it was self-defense.

I felt like I owed Cash my life. She'd made a promise to me the day I met her. She'd proven herself to be a woman of her word. She'd been consistent ever since, always there when I needed her.

She patted my leg before walking toward the door. "Cash..." I called after her. She stopped at the door, waiting for me to speak. "I owe you."

Cash took a deep breath before responding. "You don't owe me shit, Ev. You owe it to yourself to get your mind right, so you can start fresh and get this money." With that she was gone, leaving the sweet aroma of Dolce & Gabbana's Velvet Tender Oud lingering in the air.

I knew that there was nothing I could do to change the damage already done, but I still couldn't help but blame myself for Carlos' death.

Suddenly I felt a light gust of air blow across my face, causing me to tremble. Deep inside my heart, I knew it was the presence of my unborn child that Carlos caused me to miscarry two years ago. The moment both paralyzed and assured me that I would be at peace now. I always felt fortunate to be graced by the spirit of my unborn whenever I needed some uplifting.

Over time, Carlos' temper had become more and more unpredictable. As we'd drifted apart, I had dug deeper and deeper into the dark underbelly of the city's nightlife, losing myself, certain for destruction.

After meeting Cash, I learned how to eliminate the fakes immediately. I was recruited into a whole new circle and was introduced to the lavish life in an instant.

Carlos and his temper had only worsened. He couldn't stand the thought of me no longer needing him. Although he had no clue about the true position I held at Living Lavish, he wasn't pleased with the fact that the less I depended on him, the more he felt like he would lose me for good.

But Cash was right. Carlos would have rather seen me dead than walking away from the relationship. There was no other way. It was either me or him.

With this revelation, I was able to relax a bit and rest in safety with less fear and regret. But I knew I needed to get my shit in order... Change was definitely in the air!

CHAPTER EIGHT

Jersey: Bitch Got Me Fucked Up

"Yo Cash, wake up, ma! We got moves to make!" I yelled, pushing the door to her office open.

Cash's head didn't budge. It was buried underneath her arms, amongst the clutter splayed across her usually spotless desk.

Noticing bold letters on the sheet of paper resting right underneath her folded arms, I couldn't help but wonder what it was all about. *Checklist*? I thought, attempting to grab the paper from underneath her. I figured I could help a sista out. "Yo, what's this?" I asked quietly, trying to tug it without waking her.

"Jersey, get your nosey behind away from my desk, before I kick your ass," her evil ass said, before lifting her head up. Her voice was raspy and I knew she had to be drained, because she looked a hot-ass mess.

"Damn, ma. Get yourself together. We got shit to do and your ass up here, looking like a damn boogawolf!" I said, turning my nose up and smoothing my own hair in place.

Cash rolled her eyes and wiped the drool from her mouth. She pushed back from her desk, uttering a string of gibberish. "You so damn rude and disrespectful," she said, struggling to get up from her seat. She paused for a second, her head tilted in confusion and asked, "What the fuck is a 'boo—ga—wolf', Jersey?"

I plopped down on the couch and scrolled through the internet search engine on my phone. "This, bitch!" I laughed, tossing her the phone.

"Ah, hell nah! Jersey, you ain't shit!' she laughed, nearly choking on her spit. "This bitch face looks like a damn horror movie in itself," she whined.

"My point exactly. Take a look," I urged, pointing toward the mirror.

We both laughed and exchanged jokes about the big ugly broad on my Google web browser under "boogawolf," lookin' like a cock-eyed monkey with a wig on.

Cash knows she's horrible at cracking jokes, but I laughed at her ass because the shit was mad entertaining.

"Wake up! Who's the boogawolf, now?" Cash teased, nudging me awake from my catnap. She had pulled herself together rather well, looking like a million bucks and counting. I always loved it when she wore her hair down. It rested mid-back, illuminating her blonde highlights and complimenting her piercing green eyes, so well.

She wore one of her own designs, which was a hell of a choice. The dress hugged every curve Cash possessed. It was short enough to show off her honey-toned legs, yet long enough to conceal her twenty-two, tucked away snugly underneath, inside her lace teddy.

I gave her the side-eye and twisted my lips. "Well, since your ass made me wait damn near an hour, I have to say you still hold that title, Ms. Jones."

Cash pressed her lips together and did a 360-degree spin around the room. "The sexiest boogawolf you'll ever meet, you sadistic bitch," she chuckled.

Just as we finally headed toward the door, Leslie's ole ditzy ass appeared out of nowhere. I'll tell you one thing: that bitch got one more time to look at me sideways. I been itching to decorate the pavement with that bitch's face for the last three months.

"Heading out?" she asked, making my ass itch.

"Bitch, you think we standing here just for show?" I spat. I could feel Cash eying me. So, remembering where I was, I decided to pipe down.

"I'd like to think I was speaking to Cashmere. Not her Raggedy Ann pup—"

SLAP!

Before the bitch could finish her statement, I slapped fire from her ass. "Bitch, I ain't nobody's puppet. Even if I was, your ass would still never measure up, you clown-ass bitch," I criticized through clenched teeth.

I didn't give either one of them a chance to respond. I was tight. I walked off, leaving that jealous bitch holding her face in disbelief. "And close your mouth, 'fore I stick my dick in it, hoe!" I said over my shoulder, before walking through the open elevator doors.

In the car, Cash and I sat in total silence for about five minutes before the fussing began.

"You know you ain't have to slap that girl," Cash nagged, keeping her eyes on the road.

I didn't respond. Instead, I let out an exasperated sigh.

"Why you always let that bitch get to you, Jersey? She knows exactly what to do to set your ass off. You fall for it every time too," she chuckled in frustration.

We pulled up to our destination and sat in silence for a moment longer, before Cash repositioned herself to face me. "Let's be real, here. This is our establishment. It's a job. Most importantly, it's a direct reflection and representation of me. Just like any other occupation, you have to keep it professional," she said. "You can't go around slapping bitches just because you don't like them. You've got to know when to be a lady and when to be a goon. You don't have to show your hand to everyone if you know how to play your cards, ma."

I couldn't even say anything, because Cash was right. All I could do was listen and nod.

"Did you see that bitch face, though?" Cash giggled, breaking the awkward silence.

I didn't say shit at first, but picturing that shit in my head tickled me. We both burst out laughing, mimicking Leslie's facial expression at the same time.

Then, Cash got serious again. "So Jersey...you got a dick, bish?"

I looked back at her and smirked. Groping my fat ass pussy, I asked, "You wanna find out?" I stared her dead in her eyes, waiting on her response.

Cash turned up her nose. "Your ass is sick. I can't deal with you right now," she snickered, letting her head fall onto the steering wheel.

I chimed in with my usual saying, "Shiiidd..." I paused, then our eyes met.

"Bitch got me fucked up!" we chanted simultaneously, slapping hands and smacking our lips, before exiting the vehicle.

CHAPTER NINE

Cash: Blueprints & Agendas

Walking into the Sky Bar always made my head spin with expectations of good things to come. Every time I visited, I was introduced to a new venture. It's a hell of a place to recruit clients, new girls, and take care of business, all in one stop.

The sole purpose of tonight's visit was business. West Hollywood was always a great place to network in general, but this spot gave me life.

The Sky Bar is likely the longest-running rooftop bar in the L.A. area. It boasts an ivy-covered pavilion and a DJ by the pool. It hovers over the Mondrian Hotel's 18th floor, offering some of the finest views of Los Angeles.

Jersey and I waited patiently for Vic by the private cabanas and fire pits. We enjoyed the open-air nightlife scenery while the pulse of the Sky Bar thumped. It stirred a seductive energy as it quickly filled with luxurious Hollywood allure.

"You ladies having your usual?" Kay asked, appearing out of nowhere and startling me.

"I told your ass to quit sneaking up like that, Kay. You gone mess around and get 'popped', with your creepy ass," I said, with a chuckle, simulating gunshots. "Pop, pop, pop."

Kay laughed, good-naturedly.

"Yeah, the usual sounds about right," I told her.

She pulled out her notepad. "Okay. Gran Patrón Platinum on the rocks for you, and..."

We both glanced over at Jersey, but her ass was too busy vibing and dancing to *Dej Loaf*'s "Back Up."

She bobbed her head, rapping the lyrics word for word. "Yah, yah, bitch, back up off me. You don't know me, I'm too clean, I'm too g..." she paused, when she noticed us watching her. "Fuck y'all looking at?" she snapped sarcastically.

Kay and I just shook our heads and laughed at her raunchy ass. "Give her the usual too, Kay. Matter-of-fact, make that shit a double. It's been a long week," I confessed, checking the time.

"I just saw Vic walk in. She should be up shortly," Kay volunteered, obviously reading my mind.

"Good lookin'." I nodded my thanks and she skated off to fill our orders. Unable to contain myself, I chimed in with Jersey.

"...see the diff–er–ence with me, I never need niggas, ever. I'll leave 'em where I meet 'em, I ain't trippin' off no, never!" We both bobbed our heads and swayed side-to-side, appreciating the drama-free atmosphere.

It didn't take long before Vic finally showed up and cut in. "Ah, shit. Y'all hoes out here live, in the cut, as usual, I see!" she said, reaching out for some love. "Cash! What the hell you rockin'?" she asked, stepping back to check me out.

Her eyes stayed glued to my frame while I spun around, putting on a show. "This, my love, is none other than a limited edition of my new Cash'Me'er' collection."

Vic's mouth dropped, forming an "O" shape.

I did a little bop and chuckled. "Yah, yah, bitch, back up off me," I sang, slurring my words.

Jersey burst out laughing at my unsuccessful attempt. "I know, right? Slayed! She killin' the game, Vic," Jersey bragged, proudly.

"Damn right, J!" Vic nodded, in agreement.

"Too bad her ass can't hold liquor to save her life," Jersey clowned.

I twisted my lips and jokingly rolled my eyes, giving Jersey the finger. She patted my leg softly before abruptly excusing herself from the table. Paying Jersey's hasty exit no mind, Victoria plopped down across from me, making herself comfortable.

Wearing sexy curls in her dark brown hair, Victoria De'Marco was the ultimate Italian bombshell. She was one of the truest, most down-to-earth ladies that ran in my circle.

I don't have any dramatic heroism type of story for how we'd linked up. Our beginnings were actually quite simple. We met in elementary school. Over time, she became my sister from another mister, leaving us with an unbreakable bond.

Her father, Vince De'Marco, was one of the most notorious mobsters and king of the gambling realm stretching from Las Vegas to Havana. Vince hated Brains, but tolerated him and allowed him limited access in the business because he considered me something like another daughter.

"Sorry I'm late, girl. I lost track of time. Here's the agenda for tomorrow evening," Vic added, sliding over the blueprints and specifics for tomorrow's event.

I know you're probably wondering, *what the fuck do they need with blueprints?* Well, with this kind of agenda, things are likely to run more smoothly if we plan carefully. We let everyone know where they need to be and when to be there.

There's two things that will make a bitch turn on her mama if the approach is right: dick and money. So to avoid any confusion, each of the girls have an assigned area at this venue. That way, we don't have any bullshit with them competing or crossing over to the wrong territories. In turn, this allots more time to network and less time for bullshit.

Victoria, the "Party Promotor," was assigned the task of getting the guest list in order and allocating passes to the ladies for the night. Vic's job is one of the most extensive in the enterprise. To sum it up, it was her business to make sure we had full

VIP access to every event imaginable, from the album release parties all the way to the classy, upscale, private events.

Tomorrow would be the Annual Black Tie event. Everyone who was "someone" was going to be there. Living Lavish Enterprises would be in the building, making moves and networking our way up to expansion, in every aspect.

Victoria managed to pull some strings for a couple of Ev's girls to execute their respective roles. Ev's models were the sexiest, most exclusive eye candy on the scene. This made them the most valuable chattels of the night, especially with the paparazzi. Believe it or not, these industry fellas would pay Evelyn's girls five hundred dollars just for a picture.

Natalia's girls, the "Housekeeping" Crew or Cleanup Crew, depending on the logistics, would network through bartending and waitressing. They were tasked with quietly and seductively dispersing small samples of Hollywood Bliss, keeping the clients contented and horny as fuck.

Jersey, the "Publicist," would grind it out in the VIP section with Marc, while her girls scoped out the MVP's and a few other potentials that would be in the house.

Leslie, the "Accountant," would man the door. She was to flirt, pose, collect, reject, and keep her bitch-ass daddy, the head police chief, and his entourage off our asses while we racked up and cashed out.

"Let me know if you need me to make any changes. Ciera will be filling in for Ev. I'll fill in, here and there, for Natalia. So if you could just let Leslie know that she needs to have someone help her work the door and the bar to keep tabs on the dough. After that, we should be set."

"What's the deal with Natalia?" I asked, confused.

Victoria exhaled. Her body appeared to deflate before she responded. "Her brother, Javier, was found dead. Doesn't surprise me, knowing his history," she explained, sipping her drink. "The fucked up thing is, they found his mama too, shot execution style," Victoria leaned in and whispered.

My mouth dropped open in shock. "Claudia?" I asked in disbelief.

Vic pursed her lips together, nodding in confirmation. "People saying it's possibly an inside job. Natalia is shaken up and her uncle is on a mission for answers."

I shook my head. The news was astonishing. "Damn," was all I could muster up, before taking my shot of Patrón to the head.

CHAPTER TEN

Leslie: Sexual Healing

Meeting the doctor was just what I needed to relieve some stress, along with a few shots. That bitch, Jersey, had definitely crossed the line. Without her *precious* Cashmere by her side, she would be a fucking nobody in this brothel. She was doing me a great justice by showing her ass, tonight. She was making my decision to terminate her from the enterprise all but certain and the icing on the cake. I gulped down my last shot and waited patiently for the doctor to finish his call.

Dr. Palmer lay across the bed, his chestnut-brown hair tousled by his nervous habit of constantly running his fingers through it. His six-pack abs and pecs glistened under the bright lights in the room. He would periodically flex, then relax them, very comfortable with his strong, athletic build on full display.

He was talking quietly on the phone with a determined look of firm resolution on his face. Continuing his conversation, he motioned for me to come closer.

"Angela, you know I can't control the number of patients I have. I certainly can't predict when someone needs medical attention and comes to my practice for help. No, I'm not being sarcastic. Don't cry, honey. Look..."

He gripped my hair firmly as my lips wrapped around his cock, making it disappear down my throat. Speechless, he leaned back, his mouth wide open. Apparently he'd forgotten, just that quickly, that he had a listener on the other end.

"Jerry? Are you there?" the woman squealed, startling him back to reality.

Hearing the lies he fed his naïve wife gave me a rush of energy and intense pleasure. It turned me on even more. He quickly ended his call with the typical, "I love you," before letting out a loud growl.

"Fuck! You're a nasty cunt. This feels like heaven," he exaggerated. Gently, he pulled me toward his body until I was flush against him, shuddering with desire. He leaned down to nibble on my breast. I moaned, arching into him. I bit my lip provocatively and sighed. His hand rose to cup my breast, sending chills through my body. His fingers were on my nipple at once, slowly twisting it. The erotic sensations quickly increased.

The touch of his hands intoxicated my mind and body, leaving me unable to take another second of the pleasurable stimulation. Slowly I exhaled, releasing all of the day's events into his hands as I rocked against him. He thrust himself back against me, matching my rhythm. Our bodies moved together, fluid and natural. The soft music we made with our gasps and moans consumed me, as his cock dove deep inside me. I lifted myself up and dropped myself onto his hard, perfect dimensions again and whimpered.

He gripped my neck gingerly. His other hand gripped my ass tight, restraining me against him. Clutching my neck tighter, his thrusts became strong and urgent.

Unable to escape, I surrendered as my body began to shake uncontrollably. The feel of him thrashing into me, even harder than before, drove me wild. My insides began to tingle as he roughly slammed his cock deep inside of me over and over.

Arching my back, I gasped sharply as he thrust himself into me a final time, the shockwaves rippling through my body. I groaned his name. I couldn't hold myself back any longer. I came long and hard.

He joined me, his body involuntarily jerking back and forth. "Shit!" he howled. Slowing his tempo, he steadied me.

I leaned into him as he wrapped his arms around my waist, humming a warm and contented tune. I eased out of the bed and quickly dressed.

Grabbing my money envelope and keys, I let myself out, leaving quietly. Then, I hurried home to shower and prepare myself for my last meeting of the evening.

When I arrived, I saw Victoria rushing into the Sky Bar. I waited until the coast was clear before making my own entrance into the Mondrian Hotel.

My Alexander Wang dress was cut low enough to showcase my fairly new breasts and tight enough to accentuate my ass. I should've known better than to wear this dress since I wanted to remain incognito for the evening. I pressed the creases out of it before making my way over to the more secluded part of the club.

Looking over my shoulder, I noticed all eyes were on me as I strode confidently to my seat. Ordering two drinks, I waited for my meeting to begin.

"Aren't you stylish this evening?" an angelic voice sang as she brushed her fingers across my neck, sending a sudden rush of chills down my spine.

"You're late!" I retorted sharply, before she could even take her seat.

Ignoring my comment, she slid a manila envelope across the table. Our fingers brushed as I pulled the envelope toward me. I couldn't help noticing the huge diamond, reflecting off the dim lighting, on the fourth finger of her left hand. Surprisingly, the sight flooded me with uneasiness.

"What about my end of the bargain?" she questioned seductively.

Slipping the envelope into my Valentino bag, I pulled a folded slip of paper out of my corset. "Here's the address. Just do what I said and things will go smoothly," I affirmed, sliding it over to her.

She nodded, reaching out to grab the paper. Resting her hand on top of mine, she fondled my fingers, staring into my eyes. Bringing the paper up to her nose, she inhaled deeply, welcoming the sweet aroma of my Jimmy Choo perfume. After savoring the fragrance for a long moment, she grinned. "Now, for the other part of that bargain."

I gave her a trivial glance, smirked, and nodded my head toward the exit. "I'll meet you up in the room in five," I said.

She pressed the chilled drink up to her lips, finishing the contents, before pardoning herself. "That's music to my ears," she purred.

I watched her swish her hips as she began to walk away. The sight made me exceptionally horny. I chugged down the remainder of my drink. "Make it three minutes," I reconsidered.

She giggled. Turning and giving me a sexy wink, she replied, "Indeed, I will."

CHAPTER ELEVEN

Victoria: The Venue

Picking up my VIP badge, I retrieved the information off the back of it. I shot Jersey a quick text with the correct address.

Me: "Girl, your ass needs to invest in Google. Penthouse, 811 Wilshire, Suite 2100, Downtown."

Jersey: "Bish...I ain't even think about that, yo...lol."

I giggled, shaking my head at her psychotic ass. I thought back to the story Cashmere told me about Jersey and Leslie the other night. I just wish I could've witnessed the shit for myself.

Me personally, I have no issues with Leslie. I do, however, have an issue with bitches that talk shit, but can't bust a grape in a fruit fight. Leslie talks a lot of shit. So, I don't see how she would expect a bitch like Jersey to keep giving her free passes to throw reckless shade.

Bzzz...Bzzz...

My phone had been going off all night.

Cash: "Where ya at?"

Me: "Leaving in five!"

Cash: "Right behind ya!"

Starting up my 2015 Audi Q7, I switched on my cell phone's Bluetooth capabilities and dialed Natalia's number. It didn't surprise me when my call went directly to voicemail. After the beep, I left her a brief message extending my condolences and assuring her that I would be here for her every step of the way.

Natalia and I had been friends for six years, prior to her joining LLE a year ago. Since I was the one that brought her into the game, I made it my business to look out for her.

Six months after joining the enterprise, her fuck-up-for-a-brother, Javier, was released from a Texas correctional center. He'd just served a ten-year trafficking bid. After shaking up a few cities in the dirty South, he came to L.A. ready to make a name for himself. He certainly accomplished that goal before his death.

With Javier and Natalia's mother, Claudia, being the younger sister of Ricardo Escalante, the fallout was sure to be epic. Ricardo was the overseer of some of L.A.'s most well-known drug kingpins. Javier and Claudia's deaths would certainly not go unpunished.

"Damn, girl. You lookin' like a superstar!" a random voice hollered, as I stepped out of my ride.

"Fuck look like—at the right price, I could be *your* superstar, baby," I called back with a chuckle, before turning on my Louboutin heels and sashaying into the lounge.

On the twenty-first floor, Elevate Lounge always lives up to its name with a huge dance floor, relaxing ambiance, and some of the best views of downtown L.A. The six-thousand square feet of lounge space was nearly packed to capacity.

"Hola, sexy lady," a familiar voice purred, groping my ass.

I nearly jumped out of my skin when I turned and saw her face. "Natalia, you made it!" I was so excited. I screamed as we hugged, jumping up and down.

"I would never miss your big event," she assured me through her thick, Spanish accent.

Planting my hands on my hips, I solemnly consented to her decision. "I know you wouldn't, but tonight could have been an exception."

She hugged me tightly. *"Te amo, amiga,"* she whispered.

"I love you, too. Now, let's get fucked up and party, *mami!"* I ordered, pulling her by the arm as we pushed through the crowd.

Kendrick Lamar's lyrics blasted throughout the club. The place was packed and on fire, with some of the *crème de la crème* in attendance.

Some of Evelyn's girls were working the shit out of the dance floor. Others stood around just looking pretty as fuck, and raking in big bucks for the camera lights. My girl, Ev, would be proud.

Noticing Jersey on the top floor with a few of the local athletes, I began to work my way over to them. Shortly after, I spotted Jersey in deep conversation with Marc.

"That bitch done fell in love," Cash remarked, gliding over to take in the show.

"From the looks of it, *papi es* in love, too. Or he puts on a good show," Natalia countered, surprising Cash.

"Nat! Baby, how are you, my love?" Cash asked, giving Natalia a genuine welcome.

I excused myself, giving them a private moment to catch up. I needed to continue making my rounds anyway. It was imperative to make sure everyone was sticking to the agenda.

I noticed Leslie wasn't at the door. I scanned the lounge, looking for her as best I could. Just as I began to pull out my phone and call her, I see her huddled in the corner, nearly in a frenzy. I leaned over the railing to get a closer look, observing her briefly. I made a mental note to get to the bottom of her odd behavior—after everything else was determined to be on point, of course.

"Remember when we were in high school? Plotting and planning on making nights just like this happen?" Cash reminisced, as she approached and stood beside me.

"Girl, I was the one just talking shit, dreaming. You were so damn adamant. I was sure your ass was crazy," I joked, nudging her with my body.

"Well, when you have a dreamer and a believer on the same team, you have no choice but to birth a two-headed achiever!" she said.

I thought about it for a moment. Then glanced over at her in confusion. When Cash got drunk, she turned into a fake-ass Socrates. I understood her though, all too well. "See, I told you your ass was crazy," I giggled.

"Crazy for success, with my Day One sis and my top bitches in the game. We are in our prime, Vic. We about to blow UP!" she said, in the worst Martin Lawrence impersonation ever.

As the night began to wind down, I was finally able to take a breather. Chugging down a double shot of Mezzaluna, I scoped the scene.

I noticed Leslie, once again huddled in a corner. This time, she was grimacing in the opposite direction. It took me only a second to put the pieces of the puzzle together.

Trying not to jump the gun, I decided to observe a minute or two longer. My eyes had to be playing tricks on me. I snatched up another shot, perplexed. Before I knew it, the words were escaping from my lips, "Conniving bitch!"

CHAPTER TWELVE

Slick: Smoker the Joker

The club was packed. Women were everywhere, bad chicks at that. *Cash did it again*, I thought, making my way up to the VIP area. I glanced over to my right and noticed the head commissioner standing beside Jersey's fine ass.

Brains was in the building—conducting himself well, engaging in small talk with the CEO of one of L.A.'s top Fortune 500 companies. He finished up with the businessman, sending him on his way alongside one of Cash's girls.

The nigga definitely knew how to keep the cash flow pumping. Furthermore, in hindsight, I realized we really were taking this Hollywood Bliss to a whole new level. The shit is definitely in high demand.

I kept it moving. I didn't want to deal with dude at the moment. My damn insides still burned from Brains' careless antics at the warehouse.

Fools were stopping Cash left and right as she passed them. One would think she was a damn celebrity, the way they were acting. I stared at her, too. I couldn't help noticing her flawless glow. I damn near got lost in a trance admiring her from afar.

I could see why she was getting so much attention. She was just as beautiful as the day I'd met her. Brains had tried his best to keep her tucked away from a brotha, but Cash had a mind of her own. She was always sneaking me up to her room when that nigga would pass out, high and shit.

"Hold it like this, Cashmere." I stood behind her, showing her how to hold a pistol. "Hold it steady and don't flinch," I instructed her.

Even at sixteen, Cash was a natural. "Rock-a-bye, baby," she purred, her green eyes sparkling.

"What the hell you over here daydreaming about?" a soft voice whispered in my ear. Cash was the only person on the planet that could disappear out of my line of sight and sneak up on me, at the same damn time.

"Your legs, wrapped around my neck," I countered, taking a healthy swallow from my glass of Hennessy's Paradis Imperial.

"You're so damn nasty," she replied softly, nudging me. "Sorry about what happened to Claudia," she continued, offering genuine condolences.

My insides singed at the memory. I decided against responding, unsure of what would come out of my mouth. Instead, I simply poured from my own bottle and drank another shot.

"You look fly, as usual. Is that one of your designs you rockin'?" I asked, trying to make small talk.

Cash spun around, arching her back and leaned against the bar. "Indeed it is," she confirmed, with a bright smile. Her skin was so radiant it appeared to glisten underneath the lights. I could feel the whole club closing in on me as I watched her mouth move. I couldn't hear shit that came out from between her pretty-ass lips, though. I was mesmerized more and more by this chick. I couldn't seem to shake her, no matter how hard I tried.

"What's that?" she asked, with her finger planted in the middle of my shirt.

"What's *what*?" I answered with my own question, looking down.

Cash's French-manicured nail propelled up from my shirt, past my chin, and shuffled my full lips. "Still works," she teased, laughing heartily. "Looks like we have company."

Our brief exchange of friendly banter came to an abrupt end. Her mood and tone immediately changed as she adapted to the perceived threat. Cash nodded her head toward the door slightly, indicating the new arrival, as she quickly reached for her little-ass .22.

I grabbed her arm, halting her movements. "Chill Cash. It's cool," I assured her, adjusting my suit. Then, I confidently strode across the room.

"Follow me," I ordered, brushing past the unexpected guest, heading toward an isolated room in back. Shortly after entering the room, I heard footsteps from the visitor trailing behind me, followed by the slow, distinctive squeaking of the closing door.

I stood firm as I downed another shot of my drink, to the head. Before I could fully turn around to investigate, I was halted by a burner pressing up against my spine.

I had been anticipating this day for months. To my surprise, the time came sooner than I'd imagined.

"Give me one reason why I shouldn't put three holes in your head, like a bowling ball?" the gruff voice demanded.

Instinctively, I chuckled.

"Man, why the fuck you always got to fuck up the scene with yo' goof ass?" he chided good-naturedly, putting his gun back in the holster.

"'Cause you a whole goof ass right along with me, ole Miami Vice–lookin' ass, or some shit." I burst out laughing as we embraced in a brotherly hug. "I'm gone start calling yo' ass 'Smoker the Joker,'" I teased. He pulled a chair out and took a seat, refusing to entertain my comment with a response.

My older cousin, Smoke, was a professional hitta and in his prime. He'd finally made it back out to the City of Angels from Chi-Town, ready to shake some shit up, Chiraq-style.

To some, I may come across as cold and emotionally detached. If there's any truth to that, my cousin Smoke is a hundred times worse. In this game, he'd be best described as some type of evil satanic boogeyman.

When Brains' reckless ass made a mess of shit the other day, I had to come up with something fast. That nigga obviously didn't give two fucks about risking either of our lives.

Leaving me to clean up the mess, as usual, was how this alternate route came into play. Smoke was my "Plan B." This time, I ain't telling Brains' ass shit. Keeping Smoke behind the scenes would soon prove to be my best move yet.

After wrapping things up with Big Cuz, I noticed I had three missed calls and two new messages.

Brains: *"Where you at?"*

Brains: *"Meet me at the suite in an hour."*

An hour and fifteen minutes later, I let myself into the suite. Brains was so busy with his nose in the plate, he didn't even hear me come in. I lit up a blunt and the nigga still didn't budge. Finally, he pulled himself up from his nose candy, leaning his head back against the plush chair.

Standing across from him, I watched as his eyes widened as if he'd just seen a ghost. Then, he lurched from his chair like a little bitch.

Keeping my composure and trying my hardest not to laugh, I exhaled the marijuana smoke.

"The fuck, Slick! Yo' ass damn near lost yo' life tonight, sneakin' in here and shit," he ranted, reaching for his pistol. Every move he made was delayed.

"That shit gone get you 'got,' one day," I said, nodding my head at the Bliss he was snorting, humored by his outlandish remark. "What you call me over here for?" I questioned, getting to the reasoning behind the urgency in his texts.

"Damn, bruh. Took you long enough," he complained stretching out his arm, indicating he wanted help up.

I just gave the retarded muthafucka a blank stare.

Getting the hint, he finally pulled himself up. "I was starting to get worried," he admitted, sliding a safe key across the table.

"Worried, huh?" I chuckled, taking another pull from the blunt.

"Look, I know you hung up about that bitch Claudia, an—"

I gave the nigga an evil glare.

Taking the hint, he continued, recanting his initial speech. "I'm gone hang around here for a while. See what I can find out.

I need you to keep an eye out for Cash. Make sure she don't get mixed up in this shit."

The thought of something happening to Cash made me want to put some fire to this nigga right now, for even taking the risk of exposing her to some fuck shit.

"Javier's folks know the shit was an inside job," he continued.

I let out a heavy sigh. "You think?" I asked rhetorically.

Finally grasping that I wasn't with his fuckery this evening, he lifted his hands in submission. "Alright, man. You were right. I fucked..."

Before he could finish his statement, I'd drawn my pistol. Reacting to an unfamiliar sound, I had it cocked and aimed with a quickness. Ready for whatever, I aimed it toward the bathroom door as it swung open.

CHAPTER THIRTEEN

Leslie: More Than Meets the Eye

The hot shower was just what I needed to clear my head. I lingered in the steamy bathroom as long as I could, getting an earful of the conversation in the adjoining room.

Finally deciding to make an entrance, I tried to twist the door knob but my wet hands were slippery and wouldn't permit my access. The commotion on the other side of the door had me eager to find out what was going on out there. After a handful of attempts, the door eventually flung open.

"Don't move, bitch," the deceptively calm man demanded, brandishing a gun. The towel that hugged my body fell to the floor, causing me to feel extremely vulnerable. "Don't nobody want to see your fake-ass assets, bitch. Pick that towel up and move away from the damn door," he commanded, waving the gun.

"Asshole," I mumbled under my breath, snatching up the towel.

"Say something else. I'll shove this muthafucka down your throat."

Frustrated, I wrapped the towel tightly back around my body. The tension in the air was suddenly heightened as a burst of high-pitched cackling projected from across the room. I gaped at Brian in astonishment.

"Nigga, put that shit away. Leslie's ass is harmless," he declared, actually kicking his feet up and enjoying the show.

The other man's calm demeanor immediately made a turn for the worse. Enraged, he turned the gun toward Brian. "You dumb, fool-ass nigga!" the gunman explodes, clenching his teeth in fury. "You up in here, talking business while this white bitch stands on the other side of the door, listening to our every move?"

My insides cringed at his harsh, yet accurate, analysis. I waited for Brian to speak up in my defense, but he just sat there—high, useless, and duly chastised.

"What the fuck happened to you, nigga?" the man asked Brian, shooting daggers with his eyes. "Your ass is so busy sniffin' that shit, you ain't even thinkin' straight." He lowered his gun, shooting me a look of revulsion.

Lowering my eyes, I resisted any additional contact with him. In hindsight, I now wished I'd just stayed my ass in the bathroom.

He turned to walk away, uttering the most hurtful words. "You got this dull, plastic-ass, white bitch hiding up in here while your diamond is lighting up the whole scene."

Mortified, I couldn't have felt any lower in that moment. Deep inside, I knew he was right, but I would never admit it.

"I'm done cleaning up your shit, Brains. This is a mess not even I can save you from." He slammed the door behind him, causing me to jump.

Walking slowly toward the edge of the bed, I shook my head dejectedly. Before I could even sit down, Brian snapped. "The fuck yo' ass think you doin'?" He stood up, unzipping his pants. Pulling them down he ordered, "Get yo' ass over here and put this dick in your mouth."

I sucked my teeth but didn't say a word. I dropped to my knees and did exactly what my man told me to do. Causing his knees to buckle instantly, I obeyed his every order. "Yeah, bitch. Suck this dick. Slurp it. Fuck, yeah. Ahhh! Urggg," he groaned, as he came in my mouth.

I stood up, wiping the back of my hand across my lips. Then I went back into the bathroom, locking the door behind me.

Leaning against it, I replayed the words the other man had said moments earlier. As hurtful as it was, they were true. Cashmere stole the spotlight everywhere she went, and she was Brian's "diamond"—for the time being, anyway.

I felt sick to my stomach as I slid down the door, contemplating my next move. I retrieved my phone from my bag. I had a few missed calls but decided against returning them. Instead, I just shoved the phone back into my purse.

"Leslie, bring yo' ass out here, girl. Come lay next to daddy." I pulled myself together and obeyed my man once again.

Before crawling into bed with him, I pulled my hair up and prepared myself for the surge of ecstasy the Hollywood Bliss offered. I put all my frustrations to the side and partied with my man.

I was fully aware that this time with Brian was likely only temporary. I would enjoy it while I could and continue planning my next move. *Shit, there's more to me than meets the eye*, I thought to myself.

I knew how I could have the man I loved on a permanent basis. But the only way to gain full access to his heart was to eliminate his precious little "diamond," Cashmere!

"Leslie, eat your breakfast it's getting cold," Mother nagged, reading the morning paper while standing against the kitchen sink.

"I'm not hungry, Mother. May I be excused?" I whined. My head rested against the palm of one hand, while the other hand played a vicious game of hide-and-seek between my utensils and the food.

Hating the thought of wasting a perfectly good meal, Mother relented with a sigh, closing the paper. "Well, I guess Leslie," she said reluctantly, beginning to clear the table.

I rushed from the kitchen, bolting up to my room. I had called my boyfriend, Marcus, twenty-two times in the last two hours. Finally, his line was answered, but the voice on the other end sounded nothing like my high-school sweetheart.

"Look, bitch. Marcus is unavailable at the moment."

My heart plummeted down to my feet as I checked the number on the phone to make sure I had dialed correctly. My heart was thumping so hard, I thought surely it would leave an imprint on my chest.

The unfamiliar girl on the other end giggled. Immediately, I caught the annoying laugh.

"Tiana?" I asked, as my tears soaked my face.

"Don't be saying my name like you know me, bitch. I told you, he's busy. Now quit calling his damn phone, hoe."

The phone clicked in my ear as she hung up on me. I winced at the thought of another woman being with my man. And, who the fuck was she calling a "hoe?" She's the one with MY man, I thought, dashing out of the house.

Pulling up at Marcus' house, I noticed his aunt's car wasn't in the driveway. So, I quickly made my way up to the door. Before I could knock, it was flung open.

"Well, look at that...little Miss Prissy came to claim her prize," she scoffed, leaning against the door with her arms folded.

Tiana had smooth, golden-brown skin, slanted eyes, and beautiful, jet-black hair that rested at the middle of her back. She had a voluptuous, perfectly curvy body for a seventeen-year-old.

Intimidated, I immediately closed my jacket, hiding my B-cups. "Look, I didn't come for trouble, Tiana. I just came to talk to Marcus," I explained, walking up the porch steps until I was standing face-to-face with her.

Sucking her teeth, she said, "He ain't here. He went to the store to grab us something to eat. I've been mighty hungry lately, now that I'm eating for two," she stated proudly, rubbing her belly and giving me a smug, devilish grin.

Internally, I was steaming. I was so livid my head started to spin. Marcus and I were in love. We were supposed to get married in two years!

She continued to taunt me, telling me how he had been planning on leaving me to be with her and the baby. It was too much to take in all at once.

Before I knew it, I'd reached for the small statue on the porch and charged at her. "You lying bitch!" I screamed, whacking her across the head.

The force of the blow shifted her entire body and she'd fallen back into the house, instantly hitting her head against the heavy glass chest on her way down. Refusing to stop, I kicked her unconscious body in the stomach with enough exertion to pulverize the baby and every internal organ I made contact with. With pure satisfaction, I watching the blood ooze from her head and trickle down the porch stairs.

Survival instincts kicking in, I pulled my phone from my pocket and took a deep breath. Remembering techniques from my freshman drama class, I managed to muster up a few tears and a soft whimper.

"Hello? Father, I... I... I need you! A girl is dead!"

CHAPTER FOURTEEN

Cash: Fighting Temptation

I was pleased to see that the night was such a success. Everyone seemed to be having a great time, putting me in a good head space. I finally made my way up to the second level of the club where the VIP section was located.

"You better not be in here gettin' in no trouble, Cashmere Jones," Jersey whispered in my ear.

"What are you talkin' about? I ain't on nothing but this paper, girl," I stated truthfully, my voice carrying a hint of amusement. "Looks like *you're* the one trying to get into trouble," I teased, eying Marc.

"What? Girl...what? Man, Cash...c'mon, you should know betta..." Jersey couldn't lie to save her damn life. On top of that, her face turned bright red when I nodded toward Marc.

"You just better be careful, Jers," I slurred, attempting to down another shot.

Jersey snatched the drink out of my hand. "Looks like you've had enough. Time to head out," she chuckled, motioning for one of the girls to come over.

"I'm fi–ne." I could feel myself staggering, even as I snatched my arm away. But I knew it was time to go, and I couldn't fight it any longer.

The ride felt so damn long. Every time we hit a bump I felt nauseous. I reclined my seat back as the world began to spin in this brain of mine.

I know y'all want to know how I managed to kill Carlos and why I felt no shame behind it. The muthafucka was a worthless pussy, to say the least, but there was definitely more to the story. Carlos ain't the first fool I've taken out, and he definitely won't be the last. The first time, I was eighteen years old.

Brains had sent me on a run for him. I was usually the decoy, or the "leading lady," in hits, exchanges, and business meetings. Sometimes, I'd even give them a little something to look at or a wink, just as a distraction.

When it came to this hit in particular, the purpose was to send a message after some fools decided to shoot up one of the warehouse spots. Once Brains received word on who the fools were that did it, he decided that Slick and I would be the best fit for the job.

As usual, I giggled simply at the thought of his name. *That man, I tell ya...* I've never told a soul about my attraction toward him. But every time he came around, my whole body started tingling. My heart would race, and I would turn into that little girl that had stood in front of the mirror...

"Rock-a-bye, baby," I said, picturing the day I would expend my plan of vengeance on Brains. I was only sixteen years old. Slick and I had grown rather close over the years.

"Cash, you gotta loosen up. Let your body relax, and focus on your target. Muthafuckas don't take a lady as serious as they should, even when she's holding a piece. You gotta give 'em a reason to hear you, without makin' a sound."

He towered over me at 6'5", 230 pounds. He had the prettiest pearly-white teeth, deep dimples, and sexy-ass full lips. Every time he spoke, he would lick his lips, reminding me of that rapper dude, L.L.

His dreads were always neat and pulled back off of his neck. His tattoo-covered body was a turn-on in itself. His sleeve was also quite exquisite. At the center was a depiction of a regal Black queen.

His arms were cut and perfectly defined. His eyes, dark and mysterious, although his long lashes softened his look. Trust me when I say he could make a bitch damn near cum at the wink of an eye.

He was too old for me, and to him, I was just a little-ass girl. Little did he know, I would've fucked and sucked him, better than any of the old bitches he was used to fucking with.

As I stepped through the front door, I damn near broke my ankle. "Fuck...shit...damn!" I cursed, stumbling over to the sofa.

"Now you know you too damn fine to be talking like that, ma," Slick's voice rang out, startling the hell out of me. The flame at the tip of his cigar revealed his location in the darkness, as well as his sexy-ass lips.

Keeping my cool, I managed to play it off a bit. "The fuck you doin' in here, Rashad?" I questioned, slurring my words. *Fuck, Cash. Get it together*, I thought. I'd never been around Slick alone and drunk before.

"Damn. You callin' out a nigga government name, now?" he chuckled, taking a long pull from his blunt.

"Yup. Now what the fuck you doing heee–ee–re?" I screeched, stumbling my drunk ass right into his fucking lap. Trying to play it off, I snatched the blunt out of his hand.

"Cash, you don't know what to do with that, girl," he said, trying to take it out of my hand.

"That's your problem, fool...you always underestimating me." I took a long toke of the weed, 'til it burned the back of my throat. Then, I started coughing and choking and shit.

Slick took the blunt out my hands, nearly choking himself, laughing at me.

"Forget you, negro!" I sucked my teeth and sassed, motioning to get up. I must've moved too damn fast, 'cause my drunk ass fell right back down to where I'd started.

"Come on. Let me get you upstairs, Cash," Slick said, in a genuine, caring tone. He gently pushed my body upward as he stood up, towering over me. Before I could say anything, he lifted me up and cradled me in his arms. I couldn't help lying my head on his rock-hard chest.

With every step he took upstairs, I could hear his heartbeat. The tempo of his heart was music to my ears, giving me the most peaceful feeling I'd ever felt.

I woke from my slumber to see Slick across the room, staring out of the dark window. He had on a black wife beater and navy blue boxers.

Shit, did I fuck him? I wondered to myself. I mean, if we had I wouldn't be mad. I would just hate to have finally gotten some from this nigga and couldn't even remember it.

"How long have I been asleep?" I asked groggily.

"Before or after you threw up all over the place?" he asked, continuing to stare out the window.

I hadn't even noticed my clothing had been changed. "Damn. For real?" I questioned, looking down at my clothes.

"Yup. You been out for a few hours. Sun'll be up shortly," he explained softly.

I pulled the covers off my body. Then, I stood up and walked toward him. "You still watch the sun rise every morning?" I asked.

"Yup."

By this time, I was standing in front of the cocktail table, almost directly facing his chocolate body. He gazed into my eyes, and I could've sworn I busted a nut, right then and there. Trying to compose myself, I moved closer and laid my head on his chest like I did when I was a girl. This time, I was a woman, and I sure as hell hoped he noticed the difference. I wasn't sure how much longer I could hold back from him, how much longer I could fight the temptation.

"Brains wanted me to look after you for a few days. He had some shit to tend to," he said, interrupting my thoughts. I stood there in silence, not giving a fuck where Brains was. Right now, at this very moment, I stood in the presence of the only man that seemed to understand me and didn't ask or expect shit from me.

My breathing grew heavy as his hands rubbed up and down my arms. Out of nowhere, I softly kissed his chest. He just stood there. So, I kissed it over and over again.

His head tilted back in satisfaction, indicating it was okay to proceed. He gripped my waist firmly. Then, he picked me up and placed me on the cocktail table. Using his body to pry my legs open, he grabbed my hair and tugged it back, kissing me sensually from my neck down.

"You want this dick, Cash?"

I moaned my answer softly, wanting him inside of me, now. He asked the question again, this time placing his big, hard dick against my moist, purring pussy.

The ringing phone woke me from my dream. I rolled over, quickly turning toward the window looking for Slick, only to be disappointed... He was gone!

Frustrated and horny, I decided to press the ignore button on the incoming call. I turned my ass back over, pulling the covers over my head, and let the sun rise over my snoring body

CHAPTER FIFTEEN

Jersey: No Room for Love in the Brothel

I knew something was off with that Leslie bitch, son. I'm gone tell y'all like this, I don't put nothing past nobody. The other night when we were at the Sky Bar, I was in my zone enjoying the scenery when I spotted the bitch creeping through the lounge, looking all paranoid and shit. I'm not one to jump to conclusions and assume shit. So, I decided to do some investigating.

Don't get me wrong, the Sky Bar is an open spot and so is the hotel. A lot of the girls do their business at the Mondrian. So, Leslie being there wasn't really out the norm. But this bitch just looked like she was up to no-good.

Anyway, check this out. The shady heifer was at the table with a former client, Simone Pinelli. Now, that crazy chick is a whole 'nother story. But she sure as hell ain't a client that belonged to Leslie.

At LLE we don't dip, we don't dabble, and we don't test out each other's clientele. On top of all that, they were shuffling envelopes and shit across the table. The shit gave me chills because something just didn't sit right. I'm gonna make it my business to find out what the dea—

"Baby, are you going to finish or what?"

Damn, I forgot all about Marc's ass. He was sitting on the bed looking like that sexy ass Paul Walker. Marc towering over my 5′4″, 145-pound body made me melt, each and every time. Y'all not hearing me! This man is *fiiiinnne*!

Let me break it down for y'all. He's 6′1″, medium build, with the prettiest baby-blue eyes that hold me captive with their peaceful aura. I'd start tingling with just the thought of the way his scruffy beard tickled my neck. Every time he wrapped his arms around my body, I felt like I was being swept away from the earth. Literally, he would have a bitch ready to disappear. Okay?!

I was in the middle of massaging his body, head to toe, when the thought of that shady bitch interrupted my groove. I rubbed my fingers through his sandy-blonde hair. His sun-kissed highlights were just enough to complement his golden, suntanned skin.

"I'm sorry, Marc. I just got a bit spacey. You know every time I'm graced with your presence I end up on cloud nine," I lied partially. I mean, he did take me to another place. But tonight, other things were occupying my mind.

"Jersey, you sure do know what to say to keep me smiling, babygirl," he grinned, leaning his head back with his eyes closed.

Marc is 100 percent Caucasian, but the man has mad soul. On top of that, his laid-back persona tends to mellow me out.

He grabbed my hands from where they rested on his shoulders, kissing them softly. I felt my insides begin to tingle, and I hadn't even given myself the pep talk. *Shit,* I thought to myself.

"Jersey, I've been thinking," he began, breaking me out of his spell.

"What you thinking about, papa?" I asked in my sensual voice. I kissed his neck, working my hands down his chest.

His body was so damn strong and fit. Sometimes, he would book me just to hit the gym or a run on Lake Balboa. I would get wet just from watching the sweat appear on his body.

Marc kicked all those thoughts out the window when he responded with such emphasis, "Us." Right then, I was suddenly overwhelmed with uneasiness. Sensing the tension in the air, he quickly continued. "I know how you feel about these talks. I just don't understand why it makes you so nervous."

I sighed and motioned to get out of the bed.

"There she goes, running away from reality again," he jeered.

I gave him a dirty look, warning him not to push me. I hopped out of the bed and he sprang in front of me. I politely walked around his ass, taking pleasure at seeing the pure passion reflecting from his eyes.

"How long do you think you can live in this fantasy world?" he snapped.

I began to get dressed as he started toward me. Grabbing my arm, he pulled me into his body, making me horny as shit. I thought to myself, *bitch, if you don't pull it together*!

He lifted my chin up, giving me a look of desperation. "I've grown to love you, everything about you, woman. Why are you fighting us?"

Part of me wanted to fall into his arms and tell him how much I reciprocated the feelings he had for me. The other part of me wanted to slap the shit out of him, for making me feel this way.

"Look, Marc," I said, nonchalantly. "This is business. You haven't fallen in love with me. You've fallen in love with the character I play in your life. My character lives in your fantasy world along with the lies we present to the media and the rest of Hollywood to keep you relevant."

I could feel his daggered eyes staring through me. I knew what I was saying was a bunch of bullshit. He knew I didn't believe the shit that dripped from my sassy-ass lips, either. I kept my game face on, though.

Then, remembering Cash's famous words, I quickly stated the mantra. "In this game, fuckin' is a business, and my pussy is the product." I fidgeted around with my things, trying to avoid the look of pain in his eyes.

Keep it together Jersey, I thought. I planted a kiss on his soft lips. I wanted to throw him on the bed and fuck him hardcore, straight Jersey-style. Which is the reason why we're having this conversation now. Instead, I kept moving toward the door, refusing to turn and face him.

"Your ass is in love with the product," I called over my shoulder, as I opened the door. "Tonight's on me!" I declared, slamming the door behind me.

Leaning against the other side of the closed door, I felt a rare and uncommon feeling rush over me. Although I tried to shake it off, the tears rolled freely down my face. I put my hands up to my cheeks to savor those feelings.

I knew I didn't dare allow Marc into my world. So I decided to exit his instead. In this line of work, falling in love is a "no-no." I had to let it go. 'Cause we all know, there ain't no room for love in the brothel!

CHAPTER SIXTEEN

Brains: Talk is Cheap

That nigga, Slick, and his mouth is gone get him in a world of trouble. That fool really believe he got the juice when he talk that tough shit. I already know his ass think he got one up on me, last night.

To be real, I gave his ass a few passes. Only because he knows a little something about what he's saying. The man stays on top of his shit when it comes to these streets. I had no problem letting him handle that shit, leaving me to handle the real business.

Now that I got this bitch, Leslie, hooked on this dick, it shouldn't take much to put my plan in motion. "Leslie, baby, I need you to give your pops a call," I said slowly, trimming my facial hair.

The bleak look on her face pissed me the fuck off, but I knew I had to keep cool if I wanted shit to play out according to the plan.

I turned around and started toward her. "Baby, I know you don't like calling him, but just do it for daddy," I begged, running my fingers through her thick, blonde hair.

She pressed her lips into a smile. "Anything for you, daddy," she cooed in that seductive voice, making my dick hard.

I grabbed her hair forcefully, yanking her body down into a kneeling position. I didn't have to say shit; she already knew what time it was. I leaned my head back as she stuck my dick in her mouth, slurping it down again like it was a flavored Popsicle. My knees buckled, and I had to reposition myself to sit in the chair.

I lit up a cigar and ran through the plan while she sucked my dick until I exploded in her pretty little mouth. I decided to let shit simmer down a bit while I conceived my scheme and strategized on how to put the shit in motion. The sound of my phone ringing sent a rush of anxiety through my body.

"Slick, what's the word?" I asked in a composed manner.

"Shit. I checked on Cash. She was too tipsy for me to give her the run down for tomorrow's grand finale."

I shot out of my seat in a rage. "Grand finale" was the code word for "hit." "Tomorrow? The fuck you talkin' 'bout, Slick? I ain't authorize no finale!" He was out of his place, stepping into my comfort zone, and planning on bringing Cash along for the ride.

Even though I made sure I didn't get my hands dirty unless it was truly required, each hit had to be authorized by me and only me. Slick was my hitta. And he was the best I'd seen, by far. But this wasn't the protocol.

"Look, you made a mess of shit. And if you want me to clean this shit up, you gotta let me do what I need to do!"

I sighed before responding. "Why you pulling Cash in on this one, Slick? Why not Larry? Or—"

Slick quickly interjected. "As of now, Cash is the *only* one I can trust not to do some unforeseen or out-of-line shit. She knows what she's doing, and being that I trained her, she knows how to do shit the right way," he said, clearly throwing a jab toward me and my past choices of entourage members.

"What about the last time, Slick? She almost got 'got'," I reminded him, mentally kicking myself before it slithered entirely from my mouth.

"Yeah, Brains. What about last time? That was some shit you orchestrated. And to say the least, you've been a bit careless lately, too."

I couldn't say shit because he was right. Ever since I'd started dipping into the Bliss, I'd become a bit reckless, losing my level-headedness. That shit was fucking up the way I ran my business. I knew I had to get my priorities back in order before my empire fell apart, leaving Slick in the position to gladly pick up the pieces.

"Alright, genius. Make it happen. I'll check in with you in forty-eight hours, tops."

The phone clicked and the line went dead. There was nothing left to say. Now was the time to sit back and let things play themselves out. This would also give me more time to prep Leslie on what to say to her pops. I needed Leslie on my team due to the fact that I'd gotten my hands dirty in some other endeavors.

Javier had posed a huge threat to my undertakings by knowing a bit more than necessary. So I'd given him a small piece of my enterprise in order to keep things running smooth and low key. In exchange, he would deceive Ricardo and run my product for a better rate, making himself more money in the end. No one was aware of this little side deal, but us. So, his ass tried to bribe me into forming an alliance with him, like I was a pussy or some shit.

Javier had a history of being disloyal. On top of that, he was reckless. That fool had to go, and I was the one to personally do the job. It let me make a statement that only he and I could comprehend.

As for his mother, Claudia, that bitch was a snake. Anyone who would sell out their own child was sure to sell out a nigga in the streets. So, I decided to kill two birds with one stone, so to speak. It left me more time to handle the real business.

Slick was nothing more than a pawn that would be discarded in due time. Until then, I had to keep shit usual and steady.

I ain't gone lie, he threw me off with this "finale" plot. Even though I agreed to go along with it, it displeased me to think he would risk jeopardizing my other shit in the process. Guess I'll have to cross that bridge when I come to it. I'm always expecting the unexpected.

He just better hope he don't get himself mixed up and wiped out in the course of events. As for Cash, she's salvageable. Plus, I taught her how to get out of tough situations very well by leaving her to bounce back like the beast she is.

Now, I would use Leslie to drop a dime on Ricardo and his crew, effectively wiping them out the game and leaving me with clean hands and new clientele, soon to take over the streets of L.A.

I had no time to sit around and play Russian roulette talking about what needed to be done, though. I'm cut from a different cloth, the type of cloth that's cunning enough to maneuver my way through the cartel in silence.

At the end of the day, that other shit's for the birds. Talk is cheap and my playbook bypassed that method a long time ago.

CHAPTER SEVENTEEN

Slick: I'm My Own Keeper

Watching Cash sleep made me wish that I could place myself inside of her head and get her to see me the same way that I saw her. I'd been tempted to fuck the shit out of her last night, but that's not even my style. I wanted to catch her when she was fully aware of what she was doing. Besides, I ain't never been big on drunk pussy.

"I got you some ginger ale. I know yo' ass got a hangover, drunk as you was last night," I announced, walking back into the room.

Cash looked up like she'd seen a ghost. "I thought you left," she said, all dry and groggy. Even at her worst, she looked like a damn beauty queen.

"Nah. I had to make a few calls and shit. I ain't wanna wake you."

She sat up in her bed, looking me up and down. Her eyes were lit up like an L.A. night skyline.

"Damn, girl. You fine as hell."

The expression on her face let me know that I let that shit slip out, and I definitely ain't one to take shit back once it's been said.

"Shut up with the funny shit. You always trying to be a comedian on the low," she chuckled.

"Here, drink this," I offered, walking over to her with the ginger ale in one hand and crackers in the other. "Yo' ass did a number on me, last night. Throwin' up and shit all over the place."

She stared at me for a moment. Then tilted her head quizzically. "So that really happened, huh? Did anything else happen?" she asked softly.

"Now you should know better than that, Cash. If I fucked you, it's gone be memorable, even in your drunkenness," I assured her.

She chuckled, making light of the situation. I just left it where it was. I ain't never been one to brag. I leave that to the jokers with something to prove. So, I just let that shit marinate.

"Brains gone be out of town for a few days. I got a few things to handle, but if you need anything, just hit me up. I'll link up with you a little later."

She nodded her head between sips of the ginger ale. Cash never asked too many questions. Hell, come to think of it, she don't question shit when it come to business. She ain't one of

them whiny bitches either, always asking for handouts and being all kinds of needy. She holds her own in the nastiest way. I
don't mean sexually, either.

"What's the word, cuzzo?" I asked, slapping hands with
Smoke as I hopped into his jet-black Maserati, sitting on
chrome twenty-twos with the black tint. "This you?" I asked,
buckling up for the ride.

"Nah. It's the boogeyman's," he replied sarcastically, passing me the loud. I nodded my approval, realizing that my big
cousin had come up in the world.

"Chi-Town got a brotha sittin' nice," I complimented, taking a hit of the weed.

He tried his hardest to play it cool. Neither of us were
boasters, even though we came up from nothing. Never forgetting where we came from, we always kept in mind that shit can
get real, quick; and we can't take none of this shit with us when
we're gone.

"Yeah, you know." He cracked a shy grin and stroked his
chin. "So, what's the word?" he asked, getting straight to business.

"Well, we still on for tonight as planned. Just lay low for a
little bit while I put this shit in motion," I told him, taking an-

other pull from the blunt. "This that OG Kush right here, homie. This that Chi weed, all day," I said appreciatively, passing
it back to Smoke. He just nodded, as usual.

"Let me out over there. I got to take care of some stuff right
quick. Be here on time tonight, man."

We shook hands and gave each other a nod. Before I could
get out the car good, he called out to me. "Aye, you want a nigga
to lay low and shit. Man, I need some of that warm and gushy
shit to keep me entertained."

I shot him a smug grin. "Now that's some shit I can make
happen for you, cuz. I'm a hit you," I said, letting him know I'd
be in contact with that info real soon, before closing the door.

Smoke pulled up just in time. I was anxious to get the ball
rolling. Oh yeah, in case y'all haven't figured it out, Cash won't
be coming along for this ride. I just used her name because I
knew Brains wouldn't suspect shit shady with her involved. I try
to keep her out of harm's way, as much as possible.

Now, don't get me wrong, she's a beast in these streets.
Those green eyes fool these clowns every time. They don't just
resemble the color of money. Cashmere Jones will use those
pretty thangs to fuck you, assassinate your ass, and then she'd
kiss your mama at your funeral. Ya heard?

This round was all about me working my way up the ladder
and taking over the streets of L.A. I'll be damned if I sit around

and be another nigga's trigger man my whole life. Nah, I got bigger plans.

Unfortunately for him, Brains was too damn blind to see that I was even more ruthless than what he wanted to give me credit for. His ass is comfortable keeping me stagnant. We are two different breeds. He's obviously content with a nigga doing the work while he watched. I get the job done myself. That way, I know it's done right.

"Yo, you ready, man?" I asked Smoke while loading up.

He just cocked his shit back, looked at me, and gave a slight head nod.

"Let's ride."

Smoke turned up that Jeezy and let that shit bang as we rolled through the city. The city lights gave me even more energy. Just the thought of holding this heat in my hands amped me up.

Brains taking out Javier was perfect, 'cause at the end of the day, that shit would work in my favor. Just one less fool for me to eliminate.

We began cruising down Angeles Crest Highway. Riding through the quiet mountain scenery always relaxed me, putting me in a state of peacefulness. It was a lengthy drive, but well worth the views.

Soon as we pull up to the mansion, the guards swarmed us. They commanded we get out the car. Then, they patted us down—shit we'd already prepped for. The guards exchanged looks and signals. Then we were given the head nod, clearing us in through the gates. Security was mad heavy. And we were a long way out of our own territory. I could feel the anxiety trying to creep in and out of my stomach, giving me the bubble guts.

When we entered the doorway of the main house, I knew for a fact this nigga was a boss. I nodded my head in approval, scanning every inch of the place with every step. I was so engrossed in my thoughts I hadn't even noticed the sexy-ass Latina chick that popped up out of nowhere to greet us.

"Welcome. Don is right this way," she directed, giving us a pleasant smile and leading us into another area of the house. This one seemed to be the size of three rooms, built into one humongous dining area. I felt like we were on MTV cribs or some shit. There were Persian rugs on marble floors, sparkling chandeliers, and elaborate, honey-stained, paneled ceilings and walls.

I peeped Smoke checking little mama out on the low and I nudged his ass. He just looked at me and hunched his shoulders like, "Fuck it." *I definitely got to get this fool some ass, quick*! I thought, shaking my head.

Ricardo, or Don Ric, sat at the head of the six-foot table, eating what could possibly be his last meal, if shit didn't play out according to the plan. He motioned for us to sit and we both obliged. He sat erect, giving us his full attention.

"What brings you here?" he asked, looking squarely into my eyes. Before I could answer, he put his hand up, silencing me.

I gritted my teethed and immediately tensed up. I hated that shit. *I'm a grown-ass man. Can't no nigga silence...* But I adjusted my clothing and pulled myself together. I needed to stick to business. So, I let that shit roll off my shoulders.

Ricardo peered over at Smoke through squinted eyes. He tilted his head to the side and leaned back. "You look familiar," he stated, his Spanish accent stronger than I remembered.

Smoke adjusted his body posture, folding his hands in front of his lower body. As usual, he nodded, then sucked his teeth. "Yeah? I don't know you," he countered in a mild-mannered tone. Smoke never needed to raise his voice or get all worked up because his baritone voice held a lot of power in it, no matter what.

The room filled with an awkward silence as Ricardo and Smoke held their gazes on one another. Breaking the silence, Ricardo motioned to stand. Immediately, Smoke and I got ready for shit to go down, if need be.

Both of us were accompanied by two guards each. Even still, it was nothing for us to straight jack the heat right from up under their noses. On top of that, our shit was padded and ready to go. Noticing our demeanor, Ricardo stayed in his seat, giving us a sly grin of uncertainty.

"You're Smokey. You handled a few jobs for me in New York last year."

Smoke nodded his head and pinched his chin thoughtfully. "Yeah. I remember that shit," he confirmed, relaxing his posture.

"You did a hell of a job, my man. Very clean and precise." Ricardo nodded in approval.

I just sat there in awe. *This nigga is really a fucking executioner*, I thought, laughing in my head.

"So," Ricardo continued, pushing his plate to the side. "Slick, right?" he asked me, with his eyes still on Smoke. "What brings you here? You come to take me out?" he asked, letting out an amused chuckle. He slowly turned toward me.

I cleared my throat and we locked eyes for a moment. Then, we all chuckled in amusement. "Nah, my man. You know I got mad respect for you. I'm here to make you an offer you can't refuse."

CHAPTER EIGHTEEN

Evelyn: Resurrection

I lay staring at the walls, trying to clear my head and figure out a way to get out of this house, before I died from boredom. I stared at the phone as Daddy's number lit it up for the umpteenth time. I was not in the right frame of mind to speak with him. Although he didn't really care for Carlos, I couldn't seem to muster up enough courage to tell him that we were no longer together, let alone that he was dead!

"Dammit!" I screamed, loud enough for the neighbors to hear. I sat there with my head buried in my hands before one of Natalia's girls came rushing in.

"Evelyn... Ms. um...Ms. Evelyn?" she inquired, stumbling over her words. Barely speaking English, she managed to ask me if I was okay. I stared back at her for a long moment. She must have seen the torture reflecting on my face as she stood there, frozen.

"Fuck, no, I'm not okay. I have been sitting in this damn room for three days like a damn prisoner. I need some air!" My voice rose an octave with every sentence. The young woman just stood there, staring back at me in confusion. Just as I got ready to translate for her, the front door slammed, startling us both.

"Hey there, my Puerto Rican princess!" Victoria exclaimed, all bubbly and shit. She took one glance at me and dropped all her things right where she stood. "That stupid-ass, woman-beating, dog-ass..."

Before she could finish her rant, my eyes began to water. Vic rushed over to embrace me as tightly as she could. The warm sensation of her arms wrapped around me felt long over-due. I needed to be held. I needed to grieve properly and be consoled. Most of all, I needed to break free from this prison of a room.

I glanced over to see the pretty Spanish girl still at the door, nodding her head and empathizing with me. Then she quietly exited the room, closing the door softly behind her.

I exhaled deeply as Vic grabbed me by my shoulders, gently pushing me back into a resting position. "How are you, really?" she asked genuinely, her face a mask of concern.

"I'm going crazy, Vic. I mean, everything happened so fast. I didn't see this coming. My head is so fucked up right now, and I need to..."

Vic halted my rambling with a soft shush, as her finger pressed against her lips. "Shhh...shh...shh...say no more," she declared, grabbing her phone.

We sat in comfortable silence for a few moments as she fiddled around with her device. I began to feel anxious after a few more minutes dragged by. Then the loud buzzing of her phone startled us both out of our thoughts. I watched as she picked it up again, her thumbs moving swiftly over the touch screen. I ran my fingers through my hair, trying to work some of the tangles out.

Vic grinned at me. "All right, let's go!" she said, leaping to her feet. I stared at her, puzzled. "We are going to get you out of this hell hole and bring you back to life, my dear," she announced, excited.

My face lit up like a fully decorated Christmas tree. I tried to get out of bed, but my body still ached. Vic gave me a funny look, then stared at me with her nose scrunched. "Uh, well...let's get you in the shower first," she said, helping me out of the bed. "When is the last time you washed your ass, girl?" We locked eyes. Then both of us burst out laughing.

She suddenly leaned back, dramatically holding her breath. "Damn, Ev. You didn't brush that mouthpiece, either? I could've sworn I just saw green smoke wafting in the air." I shook my head, clamping my hand over my mouth, blinking apologetically at her. I was thankful that someone could make light of the situation, because I swear I needed it.

After showering, I wrapped a plush robe around my body and sat down for Victoria to work her magic. She made my make-up flawless. Without caking it on, she'd even managed to cover up every bruise. I looked like I was getting ready to rip the runway.

Putting her cosmetology license to good use, Vic managed to get every tangle out of my hair. She styled it to perfection, leaving me with enough volume to whip and flip it freely in the wind. I took a deep breath, holding back tears, refusing to make a mess of this miraculous slayage.

"Here, I got you something to slip on," she said. Then she handed me a pair of ripped skinny Adriano Goldschmied jeans, a teal tank top, and a pair of Jimmy Choo Lima cage sandals. The outfit coordinated beautifully with a white Veronica Beard blazer and a beautiful vintage twenty-two karat gold necklace. Simple, but classy and cute—just my style.

After getting dressed and accessorizing, I checked out my reflection in the mirror, and finally *felt* like the Puerto Rican princess Vic had called me. I spun around, doing a few little twists and turns, then focused my eyes on Vic. "Honey, you *did* that shit," I gushed.

She looked me over head to toe. Then, she gave me a wink. "Yeeessss! My bitch has been resurrected," she said, nodding in approval.

My smile was bright enough to show all thirty-two of my pearly whites. I was delighted that I could manage to smile after all that had happened this week.

Finally, we were ready to get gone with the wind. The feel of the breeze blowing across my face was a welcome relief. All I could think about was starting over and getting my shit right.

"I have to make a quick stop, Ev. Then our day is whatever you want to make it," Victoria promised, pursing her lips together into a smile of endearment.

I nodded my head in agreement. Hell, I didn't care if she had twenty stops. I was just happy to be out and about on this lovely day.

We pulled up at her dad's restaurant. Vic grabbed some items from the backseat and hopped out the SUV. I glanced over and couldn't help noticing the sparkle of love reflecting in her father's eyes as he greeted his only child.

Although Vic was considered a "Mafia princess," she was as down to earth as they come. "Princess" could never sum up the humble, loyal, genuine, caring individual that Vic embodied. But I'll say this: she was definitely her father's princess!

I stepped out the ride to take a quick smoke break before Vic came back to snatch it out of my hand. She would always say, " *Why the hell you smoking that shit? Your body's gonna deteriorate.*" If I didn't know any better, I would say her and Cash was really sisters, because they would both make that same face every time, scrunching up their noses. Just as I got ready to take another pull from my "cancer stick," as the girls would call it, a clean black whip swerved into the spot right next to us.

I squinted my eyes to see if I could tell who was behind the wheel, but the tint was so dark I gave up. Finally, the driver's door shot open. I damn near soaked my panties when this fine brotha stepped out the car.

He reminded me of that actor guy. You know, the one from that movie with Beyoncé. What's his name? Oh yeah. Idris Elba, that's the name of that sexy hunk of deliciousness.

I studied the guy's side profile intently. He was about 6'4", with a body to die for. His well-groomed facial hair exposed juicy lips. His smooth dark skin made me think of that song Jersey was always singing when she saw a fine chocolate brotha: "*I'm in love with the Cocoa*!"

His swag was on point and he had an authoritative air about him. He certainly wasn't from around here. To say the least, this brotha put the other tall, dark, and handsome fellas to shame.

I took a deep breath and exhaled it slowly before he noticed me eyeing him down. He glanced over at me, gave me a head nod, and walked right past my ass.

"Did he just fucking 'head nod' me?" I mumbled under my breath in disbelief. I flicked my cigarette away and hopped back into the passenger seat to finish waiting for Vic. I flipped down the visor and checked to see if my make-up was still in place.

Suddenly, I heard a light tap on my window. I thought I was losing my mind because I didn't see anyone standing there. Out the corner of my eye, I noticed someone leaning against the car in my blind spot. "Shit," I muttered, pushing the door open.

I leaned out just enough to show every bit of cleavage these B-cups could expose. With my hand raised slightly over my face, I attempted to shield the glare from the sun. I sucked my teeth and asked, as if irritated, "May I help you?"

He began chuckling lightly and that shit really did kind of irk me. "What's funny? Can I have in on the joke? I want to laugh, too," I said with a touch of drama, laying my hand on my chest.

"Nah, it's not like that, sweetheart," he responded, suddenly serious.

The bass in his voice gave me goose bumps. He was so unassuming and nonchalant, I couldn't even front. I wanted to play hard to get, but the way his ass bypassed me earlier, I nixed that shit, real quick. "Evelyn," I introduced myself, extending my hand to him.

He grabbed my hand in his and gently pulled me out of my seat. Our eyes locked briefly before he responded. "Smoke," he said with a pleasant smile, revealing soft dimples.

That shit right there took the cake. I think I fell into a state of sleep paralysis or some shit, because he shut me down for a moment. I thought to myself, *damn, poppy. You can light my fire any day!*

CHAPTER NINETEEN

Cash: The Proposition

"Is there a reason why you're in my office?" I asked, continuing to scroll through my newsfeed, not even bothering to look up.

"I've come to make amends," she chuckled nervously, annoying the hell out of me.

"Amends? Bitch, this ain't the damn cleaners. We don't mend. We don't repair. We don't restore. Need I say more?" I countered, replying to Vic's text.

"Cash, I—"

Now that she had my full attention, I viewed her with a sly grin. "Simone, you know better than that. Now, don't you?" I asked, placing my phone face down on my desk.

"Look, I...I need your help, and..."

I almost fell out my damn seat. Trying to regain my composure, I had to ask, "Bitch, have you lost your damn mind? Help? You want my fucking help?" I questioned, wide-eyed and unbelieving.

I leaned over my desk, gritting my teeth. With narrowed eyes, I let out a harsh stage whisper. "You'd better be thankful I didn't kill your ass a long time ago. You damn near put my whole agency on the line. Almost cost me my enterprise and my freedom. You conniving bitch! I would like to think I've helped you enough by letting your ass continue to breathe! Wouldn't you agree?" I asked rhetorically, picking up my phone and leaning back in my chair.

She just stood there, obviously not getting the hint. "You still here, Simone?" I asked. I couldn't help noticing how much she'd changed. She certainly looked as if life has been treating her well. I was actually a bit curious as to why she'd resurfaced again.

She looked toward my office door and the busy hallway beyond before nodding at the door and asking, "May I?"

I folded my arms underneath my breasts and sucked my teeth before giving her a nod of consent back.

"Listen, Cash—"

I gave her a biased scowl.

"Cashmere," she corrected. "I was in a messed up frame of mind a year ago. Although I'm sure it won't mean much, I just want to clarify some things. I would have never acted on the threat I made toward LLE."

Before I could chime in, she quickly added, "Please, just hear me out." I motioned for her to continue.

"Yes, things escalated rather quickly. But I fell in love and allowed that to cloud my judgment. I'm in a better place now, and I'm willing to pay double for your services."

Giving her a quizzical glare, I decided to cut to the chase. "If I believe you and decide to reinstate your services, who's to say you won't go catching feelings again? You already know Living Lavish doesn't half step. All of my girls are top-notch," I affirmed, raising a perfectly arched brow.

"Oh, trust me, Cashmere. I am fully aware of that. Thankfully, the services aren't for me," Simone said, with a wistful sigh.

Now this bitch must have really gone insane, I thought, before countering. "Look, I know our establishment is based on referrals only, but your ass isn't in a reliable position to refer anyone to the enterprise. I only considered letting your ass slide back in because you appeared to have your shit in order, but clearly..."

I took a deep breath to rein in my temper before attempting to gain a bit more clarity. "Let me pose this question: for Pete's sake, who the hell are you copping services for, Simone?" I had actually become quite amused at the antics playing out right in front of me. However, this bitch was about three seconds shy of me granting her a red nose and throwing her ass in the circus ring.

Simone's posture and tone immediately became gravely serious. She cleared her throat, releasing a throaty response. "My husband," she revealed. "Yes, I want you to service my husband," she declared.

"Sooooo...you want a threesome?" I asked hesitantly.

"No, I want him to have a one-on-one affair," she clarified firmly.

My mouth dropped into an "O" shape. Now don't get me wrong, we've had our share of unorthodox requests. This, however, sounded more like a private investigator detail than pleasure services. This was way outside the scope of what we offered in the brothel.

"I'm not sure I'm following you, Simone. What do you gain from this 'affair'?" I asked.

Simone glared into my eyes, refusing to blink. "I get what's mine!" she exclaimed.

"Elaborate," I nudged, dying to see where this shit was going.

"Well, when I met Mike he was pretty wealthy. To be honest, I couldn't care less about his money at the time. So, before we got married he insisted that I sign a prenuptial agreement, and well...I didn't see the harm..." Her voice grew lower as she trailed off and her head dropped in shame.

"Yeah, you a dumb hoe," I stated, giving her a blank stare and slow head nod.

Her head jolted up and she stared back at me, wearing a look of surprise.

"The fuck you looking at me like that for? I ain't gone baby your ass or give you any sympathy. Neither will I play the violin for your damn sob story. Your ass is *dumb, hoe!*"

Simone was clearly shocked by my response, but I refused to apologize for being honest. Pulling herself out of her seat, she pursed her lips together, forcing a smile.

"I'm willing to pay seventy-five thousand dollars, in advance. One hundred thousand in total, after the job is complete. I need to prove that he's having an affair in order for me to reap any benefits in the divorce. He has a thing for 'sisters,' if you know what I mean."

"No, I don't know what you mean," I countered. "Thanks for the entertainment—you definitely put on a good show," I said, clapping my hands and escorting her to the door.

Stopping in her tracks, Simone gave me a pleading look of desperation. "Look, I know you're not at all fond of me, but I really have no other options here. Can you just sleep on it, and I'll check in with you in a few days?"

Already beyond annoyed, I quickly agreed. Shooing her out of my office, I closed the door behind her.

I barely got the door closed before letting out an outburst of uncontrollable laughter. I laughed until my stomach muscles and cheeks ached with the effort. I had been holding that shit in the whole time that crazy bitch was in my office.

I walked around my desk, still chuckling and stretching my neck before taking my seat again. Hearing Simone's voice in the back of my head I thought, *seventy-five stacks in advance does sound rather appealing*. I didn't care much for Simone, but my feelings never got in the way of me making money.

Before I could delve further into that thought process, there was a light tapping on the door. I couldn't even answer before the damn door flung open like I was in the middle of a heist or some shit. I instantly reached for my .22 and froze.

Either I was dreaming, or the ghost of Meredith had come back to haunt me in the flesh. Regardless of which, nothing or no one could prepare me for this. One thing's for sure, shit was about to get real...quick!

CHAPTER TWENTY

Leslie: Daddy's Girl

After eavesdropping on Cash and Simone's conversation, I decided to head out for the evening. "Excuse you!" I said to the older woman that brushed past me in the main lobby.

She pulled her shades down slightly on the bridge of her nose, shooting me a disturbing scowl that sent chills down my spine. "Excused," she retorted, looking me up and down.

Normally, I'd really mess with the lady and give her a hard time by questioning her existence. Or even have her ass escorted from the building, just for the hell of it. Especially since she had obviously made an effort to try to appear incognito as she strolled through the offices of the enterprise. I just didn't have the energy to be a bitch at the moment. So I just flipped my hair and gave her a sarcastic grin as I made my exit.

If it wasn't for my love for Brian, this meeting with my father would never happen. I hated visits with my father. First of all, the man is nosey by nature, and he loves to pry in my personal affairs. I wouldn't dare show a glimpse of my real profession to him, or to my mother, for that matter.

Not that many parents would approve of my lifestyle of choice, but mine had always expected me to be something I wasn't. On top of that, I couldn't seem to find a way to rebuild the connection we'd once shared. At times I wondered, *if they were to just drop dead, would I let the cat out of the bag?* Wishful thinking, I know.

Don't get it misconstrued. My parents were always there for me, and I really did appreciate that. Once upon a time, I was my daddy's little girl. All that changed, however, when he betrayed me—right when it mattered most.

"What the hell happened, Leslie?" Father shrieked as he hurried into the house, pushing me to the side. Tiana's blood redecorated the marble flooring as her limp body lay there, badly beaten and motionless.

I'd mustered up every ounce of acting skill I possessed and produced a few straggling tears until I began weeping uncontrollably. "I...I don't know, Father. It happened so fast. I tried to save her, but..."

Father abruptly silenced me, placing his index finger over his lips, indicating I should remain quiet. Loud music and bass ricocheted throughout the neighborhood as the car zipped into the driveway, causing me to panic.

Marcus would never forgive me for what I'd done this time. I snuck a peek out of the front window and watched as Marcus got out of his car with a bag in one hand and drinks in the other. My eyes watered at the thought that Tiana was telling the truth.

"Get the hell out of here, now!" Father ordered, pointing toward the back door. Not knowing what else to do, I ran out of the house. Seconds later, I heard resounding shots.

It wasn't until hours later that I learned what happened. I was at home watching the news with my parents, when the report aired. It showed the LAPD escorting Marcus out of the house with a glaring headline. "Jealous Boyfriend Kills Pregnant Girlfriend in a Rage."

I fell to my knees and cried—genuine tears, this time. "Nooooo! What the hell did you do, Father? He was...I—he..."

Father walked toward the door, emotionless. "He was a thug, bound to end up dead or in jail. I just put a rush on the process. Thanks to you, I'll be promoted to Chief in no time," he scowled. Then he left the house, slamming the front door.

It was at the moment I realized that I hadn't just lost my first love. I had also lost the love I once had for my father, in the blink of an eye.

My mother leaned against the wall in astonishment, her hand over her mouth. I was sure she would console me, but she

didn't. She turned her back and scurried into the kitchen. The
sound of clacking dishes drowned out my weeping.

"Waiting for someone special?" I asked, standing over my
father's rigid form. He sat at the table, scrolling through his
phone and sipping his usual, Scotch neat.

"Special indeed," he replied, grasping my hand gently before I could remove it from his shoulder. He gave my hand a soft
peck before letting it go.

"You look very handsome, Father," I complimented with a
soft smile, moving over to my seat. My father's appearance had
changed somewhat since the last time I was in his presence. It
could have been the spiffy suit he sported today. He actually
looked quite dapper. I was so accustomed to seeing him in his
police uniform that I could hardly picture him without it.

"Really...you're looking quite distinguished, Father. I didn't
know you had it in you," I teased.

Father smiled and motioned the waitress over. "How's
work?" he asked, quickly changing the subject. His line of questioning annoyed me right away. I managed to hold it together
long enough to make up something pleasing to his ears.

"Work is great, Father. I'm actually being considered for a
promotion," I lied.

"Well, that's great, Leslie," he approved. In the next breath,
he pried further, asking, "What does the promotion entail?"

I shuffled around nervously in my seat for a moment, before a soft voice saved me. "Can I get you a drink?" the waitress inquired, giving me more time to come up with the right words for my inquisitive father.

"Sex-on-the-beach with lime, please," I answered. *Pun intended*, I thought, as I raised an eyebrow and gave Father a sarcastic smirk. After the waitress returned with my order, I figured it was perfect timing for me to fill my father in on the true purpose for this dinner.

I took a sip of my drink and got straight to the point. "So, Father, how's work going for you? Are you still trying to become the 'big time' police commissioner?" I joked, making light of the situation.

He let out an exasperated sigh, leaning back in his chair. As always, things became a little tense when discussing him and his work. I just played along for the sake of my own selfish incentives.

"Of course I am, Leslie," he replied, sternly. "It takes hard work to get there, you know?" he lectured, wagging his finger in my direction.

I wanted to bite it off, right then and there. Instead, I took another sip of my drink. "Well, I think I know how you can get some honorable 'recognition,' if you know what I mean..."

CHAPTER TWENTY-ONE

Cash: Diamond in the Rough

"You've got some damn nerve showing your face here," I snarled furiously through clenched teeth. I grabbed her arm, pulling her into the office and closing the door. She looked so much like Meredith, I almost forgot how enraged I was.

I narrowed my eyes at her. "All those years ago, I figured you were dead. Now that I know you aren't, I should just kill your ass myself," I hissed.

"Now, don't get beside yourself, Cashmere. You ain't too old for me to whip your tail, now. Ya hear?" Aunt Judy warned. "It's a long story, Cash—"

I folded my arms across my chest and shifted my body to the side. "I got lots of time, Judy."

She shook her head and chuckled like I'd said something funny. "Look at you, if you ain't your mama's chile—"

"Don't you dare speak about my mother after you abandoned her only child!"

Aunt Judy closed her eyes and shook her head from side to side. "I didn't abandon you, Cashmere. I would never—"

I sucked my teeth, rolling my neck. I don't know where the hell my "hood chick" attitude came from, but I sure as hell was gettin' outta body.

"Have a seat," she said.

"I'll stand," I insisted, with my lips pressed together.

"Damn it. *I said sit!*" Aunt Judy bellowed, scaring the shit out of me.

Now, I may be the HBIC at LLE, but I'm far from dumb. So, I definitely knew when I needed to fall back. With that, I scampered my ass right on over to the sofa against the window.

Aunt Judy pulled out a pack of cigarettes and tapped the box against her hand. I don't allow smoking in my office, but I decided to let the shit slide today.

She lit up her cigarette and started pacing around my office in circles. She took another puff and twisted her lips to the side, exhaling smoke into the air. "Your mama was a stubborn woman, I tell ya," she chuckled heartily. Then, she stopped in her tracks, giving me a side eye. "Yo' yella ass damn sure got it honest."

I sat in silence, my eyes facing the floor, rapidly bouncing my knees up and down.

"That shit wasn't supposed to go down like that, Cash...I—"

"I was there, Judy," I interrupted. I finally raised my eyes and saw my aunt had managed to find a seat behind my desk.

"No, baby you were at home. You were home in the—"

I shot up out of my seat. "No, I was there!" I demanded. "I saw Mama fall hard to the ground. I was tying my shoes when I heard the loud '*bang.*'" Tears fell from my eyes as I pictured that moment. "I lifted up my head and called out to her..."

"Mama? Did you hit your head, Mama?" I watched, as Mama's body slid down the wall, leaving blood smeared across the yellow paint. I ran to her, kneeling down beside her lifeless body. I shook her gently, but she didn't move. The blood worked its way toward my shoes. I shook her harder. Then noticed the hole at the top of her head.

Instantly, I knew. "No, no... Mama, don't leave me. I need you, Mama. Please, nooo," I whispered. I heard rustling on the other side of the door. Right before the door was jerked open, I grabbed Mama's special bag and ran.

I snapped out of my trance, darting my eyes over at Judy. "You were there, Aunt Judy! I heard you on the other side. Why didn't you stop it? Why didn't you save her?" I yelled, staring at her and letting the tears fall down my face.

Aunt Judy lifted her head and narrowed her eyes at me. "Are you really that damn naïve? Didn't your mama teach you nothing, Cashmere? What the hell was I supposed to do, huh?"

I walked up to the desk, hitting my hands on it, causing her to jump. "Mama taught me a whole lot. One thing was to never turn your back on family. But you left me. You think I didn't see? I saw you take money from him and drive away. You didn't see me in the window, but I saw you, and you just left me there. You left me there and turned your back on your family for some damn money!"

There was a brief silence. "How much?" I mumbled.

"What you say?" my aunt asked with a vicious scowl.

"You heard me," I replied, now locking eyes with her. "How much, damn it?"

Aunt Judy began to laugh, almost hysterically. "You narrow-minded little bitch," she retorted, catching me off guard. "You wanna know how much?" she asked, sucking her teeth. She threw a brown paper bag onto my desk. "You count it! But know this—my sister was my only family, besides you, that I had left. I would *never* take money in exchange for turning my back on her!"

She walked toward the window and lit up another cigarette. Her voice became a bit softer. "You wanna know why I left?" I tilted my head to the side and raised a brow, waiting for her to continue.

She took another pull from her cigarette. "I left for you," she said sincerely. Aunt Judy exhaled cigarette smoke and turned to look me in my face. "Meredith told me that if anything happened that day, or any other day, to run and let you be. I'd fought against it, but she insisted that was the best choice." She shook her head, twisting her face as if picturing the moment then and there. "She had a lot of faith in you," Aunt Judy smiled.

"She'd chuckle and call you her little 'Diamond in the Rough.' Meredith said the day she looked into your pretty green eyes, she knew you were a born legacy. She knew that you would be okay here, without her. She wanted you to stay and take over the enterprise she'd put together for you. I knew that I was easily next in line to go. So, I pretended to take the money in exchange for my silence."

I smacked my lips before responding back. "So why was she taking me away with her that day? We were going to leave and start over."

Judy stared back at me like this was news to her. She had no clue. *But why not?* I wondered.

"I—I don't know, Cash... All I know is what she told me. That's all I know," she murmured, waving her hands in the air.

Breaking the brief silence, she threw a wrench in the game. "Now the police done found me. They done a whole shitload of investigating the case over the years. Now they want me to be a witness."

I glared at her, now even more malicious than before. "The fuck you mean, 'witness?' Ain't no snitches in our family, Judy. Nah, we handle shit on our own."

"Girl, you must be crazy. Don't you know them people will kill you and leave you stankin' in the streets? You know who you messin' 'round with, gal?"

I chuckled, seizing the cigarette from her hand and taking a puff, knowing damn well I don't smoke.

She put her hand on my shoulder and pleaded. "Cash...come with me. Get away from here. They can prote—"

I quieted her, with my hand raised in the air. I kissed her on the cheek and ushered her toward the door.

"The thing is, Mama was right. She left the right person for the job. You ask me do I know who I'm dealin' with?" I giggled, opening the door. "I know all too well. The million-dollar question is...do *they* know who *they're* dealin' with?"

I leaned into Aunt Judy and wrapped my arms around her shoulders. "They have no fuckin' clue," I whispered in her ear before backing away, wearing a grim smile. "It's been a pleasure," I said with a nod, indicating that this visit was now over.

Aunt Judy walked out the door, pressing a folded piece of paper into my hand. "I'm not supposed to tell where I'm gonna be, but here's my address and number if you change your mind." She gave me a soft peck on my forehead. Then placed her Fendi shades over her face. "Take care of yourself, Cash. Take care!"

CHAPTER TWENTY-TWO

Brains: The Pimp in Me

I t's been two months since everything went down with Javier and Claudia. According to Leslie, her pops has been casing Ricardo's spot but hasn't seen much movement. They needed an insider, but that shit was outside of my jurisdiction indefinitely.

Slick had already set up a meeting and put the enterprise in the clear. So we could keep the Hollywood Bliss in motion without accumulating more bodies. Besides, I'm trying to maintain an enterprise, not a war zone.

"Look Brian, unless you have some major shit to pin on them, this case isn't going to stick," Leslie chirped between mouthfuls, while wrapping her sexy-ass lips around my dick.

I gripped her hair, leaning back in the chair, enjoying every minute of the bomb-ass head she was giving my ass. One thing I wasn't gone do was get lost in business talk during the pleasure process.

"Daaammn, bitch. You gone come up for air?"

Leslie didn't hold back. The bitch did all sorts of tricks with that mouth of hers.

"You like suckin' this dick, don't you?" I babbled.

She affirmed the statement with a series of sensual moans. I pushed her head down harder. Her ass ain't flinch, gag, or refute.

"Fuuuckk," I hissed, exploding in her mouth. She sucked out every drop, leaving my shit lifeless.

"Now what was that shit you was yappin' 'bout?" I asked, pushing her out the way.

She wiped the crevices of her mouth and proceeded with her notion. "My father is adamant about getting more information before he can make a move on this guy. He wants hard evidence, something that will stick."

I nodded, shooting Cash a quick text.

> Me: "Hey baby girl, just checkin on ya...daddy will be home in a few days. I got some business to wrap up, and I'll be home to wear dat ass out!"

> Cash: "Damn, daddy. You damn near made my pussy jump through the phone on yo ass. You betta watch it!"

> Me: "Damn, baby. I can't wait to see you. You miss daddy?"

"Brian, are you listening to me?" her voice wailed in my ear.

Damn. I almost forgot about Leslie's ass, until she started obnoxiously whining for my attention. Her ass was giving me a smoldering look, standing across from me with her hands on her hips.

"Bitch, can't you see me taking care of business over here?" I responded, walking toward her.

Leslie dropped her head. "I was just trying to help. I'll just go. Looks like your mind is occupied elsewhere."

I yanked her ass up by her neck, forcing her against the wall. "Where the fuck you think you goin', huh?" I asked, between clenched teeth.

Her eyes widened. Then her psychotic ass gave me a wicked grin.

"You like this shit, don't you?" I asked her, sticking my free hand up her dress.

She pursed her lips together, closing her eyes while my fingers played hide-and-go-seek in her pussy.

"Now, here's the plan," I whispered, in between soft pecks on her neck. "You're going to attend the *Bosses* party this Friday. I'll have Cash set up a VIP arrangement with Vic." She cringed at the sound of Cash's name. I didn't give a fuck either. "You turn yo 'A' game up on Ricardo. Wear something sexy and classy. Reel his ass in. Once he feels them sexy-ass lips on his dick, he gone fall weak for yo' ass."

Leslie's face switched gears again. "What? You...you want me to fuck him?"

I let up on my grip, just a little. "Nah, I want you to suck 'em off. Then, I want you to fuck 'em."

Leslie grasped my hands as I gripped her tighter. She let out an irritated sigh. "Why? You wouldn't ask your 'precious' Cashmere to fuck your rival or any of your other business endeavors now, would you?"

I raised my eyebrows. "Bitch, you questioning me? You comparing yo self to another bitch? Ain't you a tacky ass hoe," I grimaced, shoving her onto the bed. "Turn yo ass around," I hissed, flipping her over onto her belly. "Get on yo' knees."

Leslie didn't budge. I picked her ass up myself. Then, reached around and grabbed her by her throat, just enough to hold her steady. By the time I got my dick in her, she was whimpering and grasping at the sheets.

Now that I had her right where I wanted her, I was gone make her pay like she weigh, with every thrust. "Now you gone do what I tell you. Ain't you?"

She let out a moan. "Y—yes, daddy."

I thrusted deeper and stronger, pulling her head back by her hair. "And you gone suck his dick like I taught you?"

She moaned again in agreement.

"You gone make daddy proud?" I continued, fucking her senseless. This shit went on for a few minutes before her pussy came all over my dick. Refusing to let up, I fucked her harder, making her plead for mercy.

"You my bitch," I grunted. "Yo' name is Leslie! The next time you feel the need to compare yo' self to the next bitch, consider yo' self null and void thereafter." I gave one last thrust before pulling out and ejaculating all over her ass and slapping it.

"Get yo' ass in the shower. I got shit to do," I ordered. I grabbed my phone and read the last message from Cash.

Cash: "More than you know!"

Leslie's a fast talker. She knows exactly how to make shit work in her favor. I had fallen victim myself, one too many times. Now, I was using that shit to my advantage.

The pimp in me don't die. I had taught my fair share of hoes how to turn these niggas into putty, just from a whiff of that gushy shit in between them legs. Cash is one that never ceased to amaze me. She replicated, exemplified, and exceeded Meredith's style. Her ass was vicious in this game. I've yet to meet the bitch that could fuck with her, on any level.

CHAPTER TWENTY-THREE

Victoria: The More the Merrier

"You want a drink?" I asked, walking toward the fridge. Cash seemed kinda out of it this evening. "If it's on the rocks, I'll take that shit. Hell, make it a double," Cash said, lying back on the sofa, making herself at home.

"It's that bad, huh?" I asked over my shoulder. My question was met with an awkward silence. I glanced over and watched Cash play with her phone for a second before powering it off and tossing it on the table. I walked back over to her with her drink in hand. "Cash, what's up girl? You good?"

Cash took a deep breath before reaching for her drink. She knew damn well she wasn't gonna drink that shit laying back on my brand new all-white custom crocodile leather sofa, Scotchgard or not.

I raised my brow and pulled back the drink. "Hell nah, bish. You better sit your ass up before retrieving this shit," I countered, wrinkling up my nose.

Cash took a deep breath and sat up, rubbing her forehead. "Shit must be real messed up, Cash. You over there sighing and shit."

She took another deep breath, burying her head in her hands. "Aunt Judy came to visit the other day," she mumbled without looking up.

I moved in closer and had to ask, "Come again?"

Cash leaned back, the reflection from the sun landing perfectly across her golden face. Her green eyes had this marble-like glow going on. Even stressing, she was still a natural beauty, effortlessly. "Yup, you heard right," she confirmed dryly.

I sucked my teeth, plopping down on the arm of the couch. "The fuck has she been? The fuck she want from you?"

Cash just sat there, emotionless. She hunched her shoulders and replied nonchalantly. "Hell if I know. She been missing in action for eleven years. The bitch ain't even show up for Mama funeral." She sounded like she almost choked up there, for a second.

Then, she switched it up real quick, changing the subject. "That bitch, Simone, came to my office right before her ass."

Astonished, I nearly choked on my drink, spitting it across the room. "Bish, your ass is lying!" I hollered, my mouth nearly on the floor.

Cash just sipped her drink and shook her head.

Before she could fill me in, my phone rang. I checked the screen ready to press ignore. "Shit, I gotta handle this. I'll be right back, Cash," I said, picking up the phone.

"Take your time," she fanned before snatching up the controller and lying back on the sofa.

"Hello."

"Vic, I need you help for tonight."

"Help? What you talkin, boo?"

"One of *mi* girls cancel...I need chu to take her spot."

"Shit, Nat. My girls are booked for the night, baby. You try one of Ev's girls?"

"Vic, I need you for this one. They pay big time monies."

"Nat, now you know..."

"Just this one time. I send you the address. Meet me at 10:30."

Her English was horrible sometimes, I swear. "Nat?" The phone hung up. "Half English-speaking–ass," I spat before getting back to my earlier conversation.

"Ok, Cash. I'm all yours." Her ass was curled in a fetal position, fast asleep. I hadn't seen this side of her in years.

"Cashmere, I got you something."

Cash was sitting on the stoop outside of the restaurant. She didn't even bother looking up at the locket I'd gotten for her. It had been a year since Meredith's murder. Her one-year anniversary was weighing heavy on my bestie. I'd bought Cash the locket so she could always carry her mom close to her heart.

Inside was a picture that I'd taken one day, just playing around. Her and Meredith were posing in their "B-boy" stance, being silly as usual. I walked up to her from behind, gently placing the locket around her neck. Cash grabbed the engraved heart and closed her eyes.

"Yo' daddy in der?" Dana rudely interrupted, with her hands on her hips. The bitch lived right across from the restaurant and knew damn well my dad made his rounds at this time, every day.

"Nah. He left," I replied, staring her in the face.

Dana's beady eyes shifted over to Cash as she let out an annoyed sigh. Cash never once looked up. "What's up, Dana? You need something?"

Now she was acting all fidgety and shit. A few seconds later, she lifted her arms like she was in a prayer room or something. All of a sudden, two other high school chicks come running up out the blue.

"Yeah," Dana said, retrieving a blade from her back pocket. Cash just sat there, still not looking up. "You gone give me dem shoes and I want that prissy bitch's locket!" she ordered. Cash didn't shift but my ass was infuriated. Dana motioned with a head nod for her girl to grab the locket from Cash.

Cash's eyes found mine and she winked. The bitch reached for Cash's neck. Without warning, Cash clutched her arm and twisted that shit back. The chick let out loud yelp, getting Dana's attention.

At once, I kicked that bitch Dana in the leg, causing her to stumble. Cash pulled out her purple switchblade and redecorated Dana's face with all sorts of lines and curves, all while still holding onto her homegirl.

The guys from daddy's restaurant would normally shoot out to our rescue. This time, they just stood back and watched in approval.

The other girl tried to run, but I caught her, snatching her ass by her ponytail. She gasped as I made her watch my eleven-year-old friend mercilessly fuck up her girls. The other chick was still screaming 'cause Cash had cut off one of her fingers.

"Wrong one today, hoe!" Bitches knew from that day forward, Cash was not to be messed with and neither was her sis, Vic.

I'm gonna kill her. Nat didn't say nothing about a damn freak show. She knows damn well I gotta be in the right frame of mind for this shit, I thought, downing another shot of Platinum Patrón and glancing over at the big time producer parked at a table nearby. He was eying me down like nobody's business.

"Damn, ma. You sexy as fuck." The producer, Damien, squinted his eyes and licked his lips, rubbing his hands together. "Nat, you ain't tell me yo' girl was this raw. Shit, I'd wife this one," he smirked.

I licked my lips, forcing a smile, then moved toward him. Hell, it was actually more like giving his ass a runway show, the way I strode across the room. I quickly succumbed to my character's role for the evening. To be honest, he was fine as hell. So, this wasn't a complex task.

My sheer Oscar de la Renta corset dress revealed every curve imaginable on my body. I stood in front of him and gently grabbed his hand, leisurely guiding it to my hot spots. He locked his eyes onto mine, narrowing them hungrily.

"You like what you see?" I inquired.

He nodded his head up and down, still maintaining eye contact.

I slid his hand down my belly, his eyes followed. I placed them between my legs, funneling two of his fingers into my rabbit hole. Pressing my lips together, I moaned softly as my head nodded back. I warmed his hands with my juices, getting them moist enough to pull them out and bring them up to my lips.

"Tastes like candy," I purred. Then locking eyes with Nat, "Wanna taste?" I asked with a sexy grin on my face. Natalia walked over and planted her lips on mine, attempting to taste every morsel of me that I had already placed into my mouth.

Describing Natalia simply as a beautiful Mexican chicana would be an understatement. This chick was a fucking goddess. She had such an exotic look to her. She wore huge spiral curls in her sandy-brown hair, with sculpted bangs that complimented her olive skin tone. Her hazel eyes blended well with her Indian features. Her voluptuous hips complimented her flat stomach and 36 DD breasts.

Natalia swept her hair aside, her large earrings clattering. Her lips, adorned with a sparkling reddish-purple pigment, parted into a confident smile. Mesmerized by Natalia's exquisiteness, Damien had quickly been all but forgotten.

I would tell y'all that I was just sticking to my character, but to say the least, I was enjoying every single moment. This was the fifth time I'd joined in on Natalia's rendezvous. Each time, it got better and better. Tonight, Damien was paying for a show. Natalia and I would be sure to give him an all-out performance.

CHAPTER TWENTY-FOUR

Jersey: The Rest is History

"**T**he baddest one, cross this line!" the big burly chick yelled, dragging her feet across the pavement as if constructing an invisible line.

They really must think I'm some kind of damn fool. Three of 'em stood there, posted up, waiting to jump in, one-by-one. I stood there with my eyes deadlocked on the biggest one and my fist clenching my gym lock, sucking my teeth. They most definitely were buggin' if they thought I was 'bout to play hopscotch or some shit. I was 'bout to crack a bitch skull open, real talk. You feel me?

"You bad, little Red?" Bree hissed in my ear, cracking her knuckles.

"You already know, bitch!" I countered, raising my hand and clocking her ass upside her head. Before the other hoes could chime in, I just started swingin' my lock with one hand and my fist with the other.

Just as they got ready to yoke my ass up, Mister's ass lit that joint up, somethin' serious, yo. He sprayed his piece in the air and hoes scattered every which way.

"We gone fuck you up, bitch. You best watch yo' back, on my muva!" Bree yelled, holding onto the knot I'd just graced her with above her right eye.

I just smirked, tilting my head to the side and giving her the finger. "Word?"

Mister snatched me up and threw me into the passenger seat of his car. Infuriated, he'd scowled at me before slamming the door closed. I sat up straight and began fixing my hair, pulling down the visor mirror to check my face for scratches.

"Azalea!" he bellowed. I glanced over to see his face full of anger and frustration. He reached over, grabbing me forcefully by my face. "You stupid bitch," he scowled. My insides burned as he called me out my name.

"You're fucking with my money! You want to fight? You want to fuck up this moneymaker?" he asked, stroking my face up and down with his finger. "You fuck with my money, you lose your life!" he yelled, pushing my head away.

I pushed the razor swiftly from underneath my tongue. Before his snake ass could start the car, I released it into my right hand and slit his throat, with no hesitation. My eyes filled with flames as I watched him croak, holding his neck as the blood *leaked between his fingers. I had been waiting for this moment for years.*

"I guess you won't be getting that money, after all!" I said defiantly before hopping out the car and taking off around the corner.

Just as I hit the corner, I noticed the same burly chicks from earlier. They were surrounding this unfamiliar light-skinned broad. Amped up to finish what I'd started, I hopped right on in and commenced to fucking up the alleyway.

The other chick had hands, no doubt. She was laying 'em out, left and right. The "burlies" finally realized we weren't backing down and began drifting away one-by-one, leaving us out of breath. The other girl was leaning over, trying to catch her breath, with her hands resting on her knees.

Staring at me with big green eyes, she smiled and said, "Cash."

I gave her a nod. "Red." The rest is history.

"Cash, you got any cancellations you need filled, yo?" Cash had been acting kind of strange lately, but I didn't pay it too much mind. Everyone deserved some time off the high horse, every now and again.

"Cancellations?" she asked, finally lifting her head up from her phone. "What's up with Marc?" she pried.

"Shit," I said nonchalantly. "I just got a little more time, is all," I lied. Marc was my only client. But I wasn't even trying to entertain his ass, at the moment. Hearing his name still made my insides shiver with lust and memories of his stimulation.

I glanced down at my phone. Marc had tried to contact me, time-after-time, but I'd conveniently refused. He hadn't even bothered to hit me up lately. Now I'm missing his ass, like crazy.

"Jerrrsss!" Cash squealed.

"Huh...what? Girl...s0hit, my bad. My damn mind was elsewhere," I explained leaning back in the spa jacuzzi, enjoying the little down time.

"Well..." Cash began, a sly smirk on her face.

"What you on, bih?" I asked, unsure if I really wanted to know.

"I did get a new, but old...never mind that," she said, waving her hand in the air. "You remember Simone?"

My damn heart skipped a beat, or two, or maybe even three, hell. "Yeah, I remember that psycho bitch! What about her?" I asked, my face twisted.

"She wants us to...."

I interrupted. "Cash, what she want? 'Cause that bitch ain't no good, yo. And you know this."

Cash twisted her lips and exhaled. "I know Jers, but..."

"This is some bullshit," I expressed, sucking my teeth.

"You know what, Jers? I need you on this one. Just go with me to check it out. I don't trust her, either. But if her shit checks out, we're gonna be sittin' on some nice paper," she mumbled.

Something told me the shit just wasn't right, but I knew I couldn't leave her hanging like that. So I just shook my head, not even bothering to mention the fact that I had seen her and Leslie's ass in the bar that night. I just decided to make a mental note before I let the cat out the bag. I didn't wanna pour salt on the shit if it wasn't nothing to begin with.

"Aight Cash, but I'm telling you now, if shit gets outta hand I'm gone off that bitch myself, this time. Ain't no more chances. We not even supposed to be fuckin' with her 'opp' ass, no how."

Cash just gave me a half smile, blowing me a kiss. "You the real MVP, baby."

I just rolled my eyes and chuckled. "MVP, my ass. Now, tell me what this bish want from LLE."

CHAPTER TWENTY-FIVE

Leslie: A Mi Lado: By My Side

W hy did Cashmere have to stand in the way of what was meant to be between Brian and I? I wanted him badly, but I wouldn't continue to share him— or any man, for that matter. I just wanted a man that only had eyes for Leslie Davis. This situation was becoming more complex than I wanted to admit.

I stood in the back of the large room, eyeing Cashmere and Brian as they made small talk. He caught my eye and gave a slight head nod in Ricardo's direction. Little did Brian know, I had already worked my magic on Ricardo, prior to his arrival.

My black Herve Leger dress, cutout to my waist, stopped Ricardo cold. Across the room we locked gazes before he hastily made his way over to me. Oh, yeah. He was definitely circling the bait.

"I'll tell you who I am. You tell me who you are. Then, we can sit and talk. I'm Ricardo, and you are...?"

I kept my game face on, not even bothering to look his way. "I'm unavailable," I offered.

"Hello, Unavailable. How appealing. Is that an old *familia* name?" he asked, holding out his hand. "Pleased to meet you," he continued cordially.

I rolled my eyes, ignoring his hand and feeble attempt at humor. "I'll do much better when you're gone," I breathed, attempting to play hard to get.

"I'll leave, but not until you tell me your name. Come on. Fair's fair. I told you mine."

Suddenly, I felt the corners of my mouth trying to curve upward. He stood there patiently. After a while, I giggled. "You don't give up, do you? If I tell you, it may cost you," I admitted in a matter-of-fact tone.

"Oh I'll pay, alright. I promise. Now, tell me your name. I must know what to call you—especially if I'm considering asking you to dinner," he alluded. "How can I ask you to dinner if I don't know what to call you?"

I giggled and replied, "What makes you think I would go to dinner with you? Furthermore, what makes you think you can afford me?" I teased.

He moved closer to me, putting his arm around my waist. "Cut the shit. You and I both know I can afford you, and your whole agency, if I wanted. Now, will you tell me your name and stop playing this game of yours?"

The power in his voice immediately made me susceptible to him, in every way possible. I was so shockingly enthralled by his charisma, I felt my knees almost buckle. "Leslie," I purred, in the sexiest voice I could muster.

"So, Leslie, I thought maybe you and I could..." Ricardo's deep, husky voice put me in a trance. He stroked his chin, producing a curved, contagious smile.

"What were you thinking, Ricardo?" I inquired, taking a long puff from my cigarette.

"Maybe we can get out of here. Go somewhere...a little more...private," he suggested.

"Private?" I asked, innocently. "What kind of girl do you take me for?" I smiled.

"Oh no, my lovely *reina*, I don't take you for a girl at all. I take you for a ravishing, sexy, and charming *mujer*." He threw on the charm, sending chills down my spine the way the words just rolled off his tongue.

I quickly glanced over at Brian. He seemed to be captivated in his own little world with his "precious jewel," Cashmere. I gulped the rest of my drink down and forced a seductive smile. "Well, you lead and I'll follow."

Ricardo raised his brow, saying, "Ah, no can do, my lady," he smiled genuinely, holding out his hand. "No lady in my company will walk behind me. You will walk *a mi lado*, by my side."

Those words were like music to my ears. And this evening, the radio was playing my song. Although Ricardo was an assignment, for tonight, I'd take it upon myself to become someone else's prized arm candy, for my own pleasure.

It's been three weeks since the *Bosses* party. Since then, I'd spent as much time as possible in Ricardo's mansion. I lingered around, eavesdropping and reading anything I came across, gathering whatever information I could to help build this case for my true love. However, I couldn't lie and say I didn't enjoy the attention Ricardo lavished on me when I was in his presence.

I sat quietly while Ricardo finished his very gentlemanly spiel inviting me to dinner. This would be the fifth time in three weeks. I guess Brian did, in fact, know exactly what type of woman Ricardo would take to.

Just as I got ready to respond, there came a light knock at the door.

"Come in," Ricardo ordered.

"*Bueno, señor.* Your ten o'clock is here," the man said. Then, he walked over to Ricardo and whispered something in his ear. I almost sprained my neck trying to listen, but the Spanish accent completely threw me off.

"Leslie, my darling, I have some important things that re-quire my attention at the moment."

I gingerly took a sip from my wine glass. "Would you like me to go, Ricardo?" I asked, already knowing the answer.

"Of course not, *señorita*. This won't take very long. Besides, you should be getting ready for round two." He winked, plant-ing a kiss full of promise on my check.

"Don't keep us waiting," I sang, caressing my vagina, giving him a brief masturbating porn show.

"*Si, mamacita.* I like your style. *Hasta más tarde,*" he said, licking his lips and nodding his head. Then he slowly walked out, closing the door gently behind him.

I waited all of five minutes before opening the door, trying not to capture the attention of his wingman. I tiptoed over to the spiral staircase, crouching down to remain unseen.

"*Ya esta el ganado listo?*" Ricardo asked calmly, smoking his cigar. I thought my Spanish was getting a little rusty.

Is the cattle ready? I thought to myself, confused. I eavesdropped a little more to see if I could get a bit more clarity.

"*Si, ya esta listo.*"

"It is ready," I whispered to myself, nodding my head up and down. *Ah, "cattle" must be code*, I thought. "Ok, Ricardo baby, I need a date and time," I whispered anxiously.

"*Cuando lo puedo recoger?*" Ricardo asked.

Good job, baby. Keep it straight and to the point, I cheered silently.

"*El Sabado, son las cinco de la tarde, en las Colinas.*"

"Five o'clock, Saturday...at...the hill... Bingo!" It all seemed so simple. Now, I just had to get the hell out of here without shaking things up. I lifted myself up slowly, watching as the big Spanish guy shook Ricardo's hand, sealing the deal.

Before I could even stand up fully, I was stunned to see a familiar face, right in the front of the den. I damn near pissed myself. I shook my head from side-to-side to make sure my vision wasn't distorted.

"No fucking *way!*" I spat. I clamped my hand over my mouth, silently cursing several more times as I stubbed my toe backing away. I let out a silent cry, then began racking my brain to come up with a fast strategy to get the hell out of dodge.

CHAPTER TWENTY-SIX

Smoke: Unfinished Business

I didn't mean to end the meeting so suddenly, but *some* shit would have to wait over other priorities. I slipped out the back entryway, the same way this bitch probably thought she would make her own discreet departure from. Nah, not on my watch. I pay attention to everything.

I watched her creepin' around like her white ass was invisible or some shit. I saw when she crouched down, ear hustlin' too. I even calculated the exact amount of time it would take before her sneaky ass would see my face. I didn't even have to look at her. I could smell the fear oozing through her pores when she finally came to the realization of who I was.

I stood at the back exit, watching her tiptoe out the door. I quickly snatched her up, put my hands around her mouth, and drug her a few feet away. "Bitch, you better not move," I whispered harshly before firmly pressing the chloroform-soaked terry cloth towel around her face until she passed out.

I drove to the vacant spot in Inglewood that I'd used on a number of occasions since I'd been here on this operation. Tonight, Leslie would serve a special purpose here, one of my own.

I yoked her up out my ride and drug her into the building, forcing her sluggish body up against the wall. I held her up with my hands wrapped around her neck. Leslie's eyes fluttered momentarily before they opened wide like she'd just seen a fucking ghost.

Her lips quivered as she opened her mouth to utter up some bullshit. "Who are you? What do you want from me?" she asked, pretending to be clueless.

I managed to remain calm, even though I wanted to wring her neck right then and there. Nah, I needed answers from this snake-ass bitch. "Oh, so now you don't know who I am?" I asked, clenching my teeth. She must've seen the fury in my eyes because I could feel her body shudder.

"I swear I didn't know... I didn't mean it..." she sputtered.

I tightened my grip. "I thought you didn't know who I was?" I asked, softening my eyes. I'm sure the change in my expression confused her. That's exactly how I liked it. The terror on her face made my dick rise but I wouldn't fuck this bitch with a sick dick.

"I swear to you, it wasn't—"

I pushed her back against the wall in a rage. "Wasn't *what*, Leslie? Huh?"

"Marcus, look...it was an accident. I swear."

I backed away, scratching my head with my gun like a mad man.

"You—you did that shit on purpose, bitch! You killed my girl and my unborn baby. Then you and yo' bitch-ass father let *me* take the fall for that shit!" I could feel the rage funneling inside of me.

Leslie motioned to walk toward me. I aimed the gun straight at her face. "Bitch, don't you move," I grimaced. "You took life from me. Fuck that...you took *lives* from me. You just couldn't accept the fact that our shit was over. Yo' ass always had to have shit yo' way. But I never once imagined you'd take my life from me in more ways than one. You took away my chance to be a father *and* my freedom, all in one whop. You a reckless bitch, Leslie, and yo' ass don't deserve to breathe." I could feel my blood boiling in my body. I cocked my shit back.

"Waitttttttt!" she screamed with her hands splayed out in front of her.

Now, normally a muthafucka wouldn't have the chance to plead for their life, but this isn't my normal assassination process either. I had no ties to my other victims. There were no back stories or personal vendettas. This bitch actually had my heart at one point. My love for her would be my downfall time-after-time. All the way up until I had to cut ties from her crazy ass, she still led me into the pits of hell.

My eyes softened as I watched her big blue eyes tear up, but I still managed to let her hear the seriousness in my tone. "You want the floor, bitch? You got ten seconds before I end this shit, here and now."

Leslie stood upright and adjusted her clothing. Then, she cleared her throat and said, "You want to kill me, Marcus? Well it wouldn't be the first time."

I shot her a dubious look but let her continue.

"You killed me a long time ago when you took away our chance of being a family. You played me, Marcus, and like a coward you let your sidepiece do the dirty work."

I cocked my neck to the side. "Nah, you wrong. You were the side bitch, not Tiana," I lied, intent on tormenting her even more.

It was obvious that my words hurt her to the core. Unexpectedly, her expression abruptly shifted and her voice turned cold. "Well, that says a lot. You're not only a coward, you're a liar, too." Her words cut like swords.

"Yes, I killed your little 'girlfriend,' and I'd do it again if I had to. But let's face it, Marcus, *you're* the one responsible for their deaths. Their blood is on your hands too, Marcus."

I aimed my gun at her and narrowed my eyes.

"But I didn't set you up. That was all my father's doing. I panicked, and he told me to run. It wasn't until—"

I quickly interjected. "Time's up, bitch," I stated.

"I was carrying your baby too, Marcus. That's why I was calling you that day."

I could feel a lump forming in my throat. "Don't fuckin' insult my intelligence," I warned.

Leslie pressed her lips together and exhaled deeply. "Look, what do I have to lose, Marcus? You're going to kill me anyway, right?" she tested. "I came to visit you. They said you were shipped away to some military school or something," Leslie said, waving her hands about in frustration.

She was correct, so far. So I let her finish.

"I tried to hide it as long as I could. By the time my father caught wind that I wasn't just gaining a few pounds, it was too late to terminate the pregnancy."

That damn lump formed in my throat again. *What the fuck was she saying?* "What you mean, 'too late?' You saying what, Les?" I hadn't called her that in over ten years.

"I'm saying...you're a father, Marcus! My child, *our* child... Father...he...he made me give him away." Leslie began to weep. "I hate him every single day for that. He said it would be a bastard baby and...that we were better off apart, with him not having a father and all."

My eyes began to water. I couldn't believe what I was hearing. "He?" I whispered.

"Yes, Marcus. He's thirteen now, and I know where he is. I can help you connect with him. Just please don't kill me. Let me make this up to you!"

CHAPTER TWENTY-SEVEN

Victoria: Caught Red-handed

"Evelyn, you're full of shit! It's been two months since you've been seeing this 'mystery guy.' How long do you plan on keeping him a damn secret?" I asked, waving the cloud of smoke from my face.

"Damn, Victoria De'Marco. Must you know *all* my endeavors?" Ev chuckled, coughing on her cancer stick.

She rubbed her hands through her fresh, new, honey-blonde colored hair. The heat was blazing as we strolled along the strip waiting for Jersey to meet us for coffee. Evelyn had such a healthy glow about her ever since she'd started dating this mystery guy. I didn't know who he was, but he was sure keeping my girl happy. That gave him hella points, in my book.

"You damn right. I need to know everything, Evelyn. I have to make sure he's not the damn boogeyman or some shit..." I teased.

Evelyn took another puff, irritating the hell out of me. "Oh, he's the boogeyman, alright!" she mocked. "He makes *all* my insides quiver," she laughed, doing some kind of bootlegged Macarena.

I wrinkled up my nose. "You ain't shit. Does he ask any questions about your work?"

Evelyn got real quiet.

"You didn't?"

"Vic...I couldn't help it. We were pillow-talking and sharing stories. It just felt so—"

I interrupted her. "You know damn well we keep this operation low-key. How else do you suppose we stay the fuck out of jail and keep our names clean? If your ass gets hauled in, how the hell do you think your lawyer of a father would take the news, huh?"

Evelyn sucked her teeth. "Vic, you didn't even have to go there. Damn!"

I stopped dead in my tracks. "Look, you're my girl and I love you for that. But if our business starts leaking and my name is drug through the shit, I'm gonna literally drag your ass through the fucking mud. I'll leave your ass there, too. Business is business. Don't start getting your business and your emotions mixed up in the same bag, you hear?"

Evelyn nodded her head, shamed. "Got it..." she mumbled.

"Now, tell me all about him. And don't you leave out a single detail!"

After my meeting with the girls, I decided to get some daddy-daughter time in with my pops before he went out of town on business. I love my father more than words can say. Although, trust and believe, being the daughter of a mobster isn't filled with glamour and crystal stairs. I've witnessed shit that would offend Lucifer himself, but I wouldn't trade my pops in to save my life.

We have a great relationship. On top of that, my dad is still a good-looking, single, Italian fella. With all the floozies running in and out of his restaurant, my mother left when I was just twelve years old, never to return.

"Victoria, let's go! You're not packing fast enough!" My mother whispered, trying not to wake Papa.

I lagged behind, full of confusion and rebellion, all rolled into one. "Mama, why do we have to go without Papa? I can't leave my papa here. He's going to be lonely without me."

My mother grabbed me angrily by my shoulders. Her eyes were bloodshot red. "Victoria, your father is a very dangerous man. He can kill with no shame!"

I pulled away from my mother, giving her a smoldering look. "Papa never killed anyone. He is a good man. He loves me... You're just jealous." My mother raised her hand and hauled it back to slap me. Just then, Papa appeared out of nowhere and grasped her hand calmly.

He whispered something into Mama's ear as she stood there frozen. "Carlita, if you would like to leave the premises, I have no problem with Nicolas escorting you out of here. But you will NOT take away my daughter," he said, his voice cold with venom.

Mama stared at my papa and then spat in his face. Calmly, he passed her over to Nicholas without another word. Then he knelt down and opened his arms for me. I ran to him, and he wrapped his arms around my petite body.

"Papa?" I whispered.

"Yes, my princess?"

I pulled away from him slightly and stared him in his eyes. "What's a 'mafia?'"

Papa remained calm and stood upright, pulling out his big cigar before responding. "It's my family—our family—a family that sticks together by any means. We don't cross one another. Loyalty is everything."

My father broke down the history of the Italian legacy, the mafia's origin—how they started out as immigrants and had to earn their respect before forming alliances and becoming a larger organization, and how they did what they had to do for their families.

I stood there like a little soldier girl and gazed up into my papa's eyes. "Well Papa, I'll never leave your side, and I'll never judge you!"

And I never did!

I kissed my papa goodbye, wishing him a safe trip. Exiting the restaurant, I noticed Leslie getting out of her car and heading into the hotel across the street. She had been acting real anxious lately. Today, I was gonna get to the bottom of what was really going on.

I hadn't forgotten the night of the Black Tie Event, either. That night I saw Brains whisper something in her ear. Seconds later, they both disappeared in the wind. I'd made a mental note to check it out.

I guess my event calendar just gave me a friendly reminder today. Especially when right at that moment, I saw Brains pull in behind Leslie.

Oh, their asses were caught, red handed!

CHAPTER TWENTY-EIGHT

Brains: It's All About Compliance

Leslie walked reluctantly into the room, irritating the shit out of me. I kept my cool and sat on the edge of the bed. I pulled out a little taste of the Bliss, motioning for her to come join me. As she walked over, I could see her body visibly relax a little. "You got something for me?" I asked, stroking her blonde hair gently.

Leslie nodded her head slowly. Then she swiped her nose and responded. "Yeah. I got you something," she said, giving me attitude.

I bit my tongue and took a deep breath. I really wanted to smash the bitch face in.

"Everything will go down this Saturday at 5:00. My father is already handling his part," she continued, not even bothering to look my way.

"That's my girl," I praised, stroking the side of her face. She began to pull away from my touch. So I grabbed a fistful of her hair, yanking her back toward me.

"The fuck wrong with you?" I questioned with a scowl, now reaching my breaking point. "Yo' ass had a change of heart? You spent less than a month outta my presence and you smelling yo' self now?" I gripped her tighter. "Or you done fell in love with the trick?"

Leslie pressed her lips together tightly as tears rolled down her face.

Before she could muster up a single word, I decided to really get up under her skin, show her just who the fuck the boss is here. I released her hair and shoved her head into the mattress.

"You was right. I shouldn't have sent yo' fickle ass to do a real woman's job. I figured since you wanted Cash's spot so bad, you could put in the work. But nah, I had too much faith in yo' ditzy ass."

Leslie's body jolted upright as a dark, brooding expression covered her face. She let out a deep sigh. "No, Brian. I would never turn on you. I love you!" She began to whimper.

I turned my back to her and lit up a cigar. "Nah, bitch. Yo' ass over there looking like you just lost yo' best friend and shit. You ain't ready," I tormented her. Taking a pull from my cigar, I turned to face her.

She quickly started explaining herself. "I've got a lot of things going on, Brian... I... I need you. I swear, I would never betray you."

Leslie purred like a Persian kitten as she crawled over to me, turning me on. I gripped my dick as I watched the show briefly until she got close enough. Then I knelt down before her, giving her a smoldering glare. I wrapped my hands around her neck and pulled her up to her feet.

"Well, yo' ass better start complying, then. I don't need no needy-ass, weak-minded bitch in my corner, on my team, or in my presence. Especially since I'm gone be running these streets. I can't have you questioning my motives, giving me lip and shit."

I couldn't have Leslie fucking up my plans. So I was rough enough to put her back in line, but not too rough, causing me or her to lose sight of what I really needed from her. Trust and believe, after this shit was over she would be cast-off, in the worst way.

"I got shit to do. So I need you to get yo' ass back to work before somebody start suspecting shit," I hissed.

"I thought we would spend the evening..."

I gave her a wide-eyed stare of disbelief and said, "Compliance, bitch. Compliance."

Leslie nodded her head obediently and dismissed herself from my presence.

Just as I'm congratulating myself, thinking, *that shit went smoothly*, I hear a light tapping at the door. Snatching open the door, I yelled, "The fuck I say about compliance, Les—"

Victoria's eyes locked onto mine.

I stood there wearing a deadpan expression, waiting to see if anyone else was tagging along for the ride. When I saw it was just her, I shook off the element of surprise, adapting swiftly.

"Fuck you want? You got the wrong room, don't you?" I asked wittily, backing away from the door so she could step in.

"Really? Brains, this is what you do to my girl?" she asked, shaking her head.

I closed the door behind her. "Man, I don't know what yo' delusional ass here barkin' 'bout," I dismissed, taking a pull from my cigar.

She stood there sucking her teeth. Then she folded her arms, asking, "So, I'm just seeing shit, huh?" She sighed, vexed. "Leslie, though?"

I was about sick of her nagging in my ear about my activities. I stroked my goatee slowly and managed to remain cool.

"You must got some clients over here or some shit?" I drawled, brushing past her. "Or you gone cut out the middle man and pay me in person today?" I badgered.

Victoria followed right behind, hounding me all in my ear. "You think this shit is a joke? You playing my girl, with Les! Your ass is foul..."

Raising my eyebrow, I blew out a gust of smoke in her face, knowing how much she hated it. "Aye, you betta think again before questioning me," I warned.

She stood there, waving the cloud of smoke out of her direction. She walked up a bit closer, standing firm with her arms folded, tapping her foot against the floor. "You got some nerve...I figured you had more respect for my girl. I hate to have to relay this shit to her, but you leave me no fucking choice," she threatened, before doing a 180-degree turn and heading toward the door.

Before I could catch myself, I snatched her ass up and slammed her against the wall, gripping her by her throat. "Bitch, the fuck you talkin' 'bout, huh?"

Not at all frightened, Vic stared back at me with the cold, cynical eyes of indifference. Then, she gave me a sly grin. "You might wanna get your hands from around my neck, you heartless bastard!" she hissed, kneeing me in the groin.

"You disrespectful bitch!" I seethed, hunkered over in pain.

"Bitch? Oh, I got your bitch!" she thundered, reaching for the machete I had planted on the nightstand.

She darted toward me with the big knife. *This bitch done lost her mind, pulling a weapon on me,* I thought. I had to be gettin' soft, 'cause these hoes had truly been testin' my gangsta, and that shit ain't gone fly. Mafia, or not, I refused to conform into a pussy.

I instinctively went into beast mode, returning the motion. I reached for her wrist but she was too swift and managed to swipe my abdomen. Adrenaline pumping, I didn't even realize the extremity of the wound. I raged, frantically reaching for the knife.

Catching hold of her wrist, we struggled momentarily. I had clearly underestimated her strength. Finally, I managed to retrieve the knife from her grip.

I pushed her back against the wall with one hand as my other, on reflex, swiped across her neck, causing her body to slide down the wall. I stood back, astonished, watching her choke on the gurgling blood and grasp at her neck in shock. Her eyes filled with deep anguish as blood gushed through her well-manicured fingers.

CHAPTER TWENTY-NINE
Cash: Until Death

I sat outside of the restaurant at the forum for forty-five minutes, contemplating how I wanted to approach Simone's husband. Before I could get a clear visual of the girl I would use for the job, I needed to learn as much as I could about him. I wanted to ensure this job went smoothly.

I had been watching him for a week. Every time I saw him, I was hit by an unexpected surge of anxiety. Each time, I ignored it.

I mean, this task was out of the norm for the agency. Usually, our clients were fully aware of what type of services we provided and often participated in the selection process. Against my better judgment, I had taken on the mission at hand.

My thoughts were interrupted as a basketball bounced against my Louboutin flats. As I leaned over to retrieve the ball, a pair of tawny-colored hands suddenly collided with my own. The boy just stood there staring, like he was frozen to the spot. Noticing my ample cleavage had obviously garnered his attention, I pulled back, bringing the ball with me.

"Marcus, apologize to the nice lady," a deep voice ordered.

Before the boy could respond, I interjected. "No worries," I said, smiling sweetly at the handsome teenager. I turned my head in the direction of the man, obviously with the child, and couldn't believe I hadn't noticed it was Simone's husband.

He extended his hand. "Mike," he introduced himself.

Caught off guard, I cleared my throat and returned the gesture. "Daphne..." I lied.

"Daphne, you live on this side of town? I'm sure I would have noticed such a dazzling—"

I chimed in, interrupting him. "No. I'm here on...business. I was just about done," I assured him, moving to get up from my seat. Standing upright, I locked gazes with the man. Something in his greenish eyes gave me a dose of *déjà vu*. Brushing off the feeling, I glanced over at the boy. "Is that your son?" I pried, seeing no resemblance.

"Yes he is," he beamed proudly. I never knew Simone had any children. Now, I was taken aback. The boy didn't look like either of them.

Seemingly reading my thoughts, Mike chuckled. "He's adopted. I've had him since he was a day old. Aside from blood, he's all mine," he winked.

I pressed my lips together into a friendly smile. "Indeed, he is."

The vibration from my phone broke the awkwardness lingering in the air. I glanced at the number and made a mental note to return the call a little later. Seconds later, a voicemail notification came through. I thumbed through a few messages, then silenced my phone.

"Busy lady, I see," he meddled.

Dismissing his intent to extend the conversation, I let out a restless sigh. "I guess I better get going..." I cued, gathering my things. I fumbled and dropped a few items in my haste.

Simultaneously, we both bent over to pick up the items. He raised an eyebrow as he scanned over my business card. "Living Lavish...?"

I kindly retrieved the card from his hand without panic. "I'll take that," I said with a smile, before turning and heading toward Ms. Porsche.

I could feel his eyes on me as I walked toward my car. I opened the passenger door and placed my items on the seat. Still sensing I had an audience, I closed the door and turned to see both of them with their necks craned and their eyes locked dead on my ass...ets, so to speak.

"Well, I'll let you get to it," he smiled.

I nodded and smiled back, knowingly. Then, I waved at them both before getting into my car. Leaving them both frozen in a state of awe and admiration—no doubt, watching me disappear in the wind.

"Call Vic," I chirped to Ms. Porsche's voice-recognition Bluetooth software. The ringing sound pierced my eardrums as it blared through the speakers of my car's stereo system. The call went to voicemail just as I turned the corner, cursing to myself at the sight of a dozen police cars and ambulances.

Trapped in the midst of chaos, I decided to scroll down my newsfeed for some form of entertainment while killing time. "Oh, hell nah. Why the fuck would she have those shoes on with that dress?" I pinched my screen to zoom in. "Is that her fuckin' bra? Well, that's tacky. Ugh," I shook my head in disgust, scrolling past the epic fails and horrific attempts at fashion. I invited a few of the girls to like my boutique page and logged out. I couldn't stomach social media for too long—only small doses at a time.

Traffic still waylaid, I watched as the paramedics wheeled out a gurney. The white sheet concealed the body, but blood seeped through, sending chills down my spine. The shoes, dangling over the edge of the gurney, revealed the gender. Then, I saw a limp arm fall from underneath the sheet. I swallowed hard, suddenly overcome with a rush of uneasiness. I jumped out of my car, not even bothering to close the door behind me.

"Ma'am?" I heard a voice call out.

"You can't go over there!" another chimed in.

I saw the mouths of the officers moving, but felt like everything was moving in slow motion. My head was spinning. I couldn't seem to pull myself together enough to snap into full speed.

Noticing the charms dangling from her wrist, my knees buckled, both in fury and distress. Attempting to stand, I immediately became nauseous. I tried to scream out, but had no voice.

"Are you okay?" I thought I heard a voice ask.

"Miss...can you hear me?"

The voices begin to fade. My heart beat so hard, it felt like it was smacking me in the face.

"Vic, you can't be all extra loud and shit. We gotta stay low-key," I whispered.

"Low-key? You act like we goin' on a damn heist or somethin'."

I gave her a mocking grin. "Just move ya ass," I ordered, as we tiptoed through the back door of Ray's barber shop.

I'd heard a few of the football players talking about getting faded here and some other superficial bullshit. I had been scoping the spot out for about two weeks. It was apparent that this barbershop was just a decoy for the brothel that was racking up the big bucks. We watched a couple of exchanges and even got a chance to catch a sneak peak of the show.

"Cash, what they doing?"

I stared at Vic sideways and smacked my lips. "Fuckin'," I spat pointedly. "Vic, this is what we gone do one day, but better!

We damn sure not gone do it in the back of some raggedy-ass barber shop."

She shot me a look of revulsion. "Fuck that...I ain't on that shit, Cash."

I dismissed her immature mindset and kept my eyes planted on what was taking place in front of me. "So, you just gone be out here fuckin' for free, huh? Ain't no good in that shit. These clowns gotta pay to play, and that's that."

Vic rolled her eyes and twisted up her lips. "Well, I'll just book the appointments and shit, plan the venues, and fill them shits up."

I nodded in approval. "That sounds like a plan, Vic. Just watch. I got a strategy." I pulled a small jewelry box out of my pocket. "Gimme your hand."

Vic stuck out her hand, apprehensively. I pulled out the matching charms, one embedded with LLE and the other with the money symbol, but this symbol had two lines forming into a 'V.'

"Never take it off. This is our emblem of our sisterhood."

A lone tear rolled down Vic's cheek as she nodded in agreement. "Until death," she said.

"Until death," I repeated.

CHAPTER THIRTY

Cash: I Am My Sister's Keeper

Everything felt like it was shifting in my head. My sister, my ace, and my right hand had been ruthlessly snatched away. The crumpled papers flooded my office space. I couldn't even manage to come up with the right words to say at her funeral. Everything was closing in on me. I felt like I was underwater and couldn't come up for air, not even for my girl's final departure.

A light tap at the door disturbed my thoughts. I decided to ignore it and instead kept working on Vic's eulogy. "Cash, can I come in, ma?" Jersey's voice was music to my ears. It was like hearing a powerful love song after experiencing a broken heart.

As the doorknob turned, my body weakened. Immediately, I regained my composure, not showing any signs of weakness. "Hey, Jers. What you got for me?" I asked, reluctantly looking up.

"Well...first, I got you something to put on your stomach. I'm pretty sure you haven't eaten. From the looks of it, ya ass ain't slept, either." she said, her mouth twisted.

"I got a shitload of things to do, Jers. Speaking of which...I need you to run me over to Vic's. I need to grab a few things."

"Alright, bet. But first, you need to feed ya face. That's not a request."

When we arrived at Vic's, part of me still expected to see her peek through the blinds or come out doing some kind of off-rhythm dance, with her crazy ass. The reality of it all was that she would never open that door or peek through those blinds again.

I walked into her house using my spare key. It was so quiet and peaceful. On the nightstand sat a photograph of Vic and I, from the night of our senior prom. I picked it up and rubbed my fingers across the glass frame, tracing the outline of Vic's face.

"Keep still, dammit. Who in the hell told you to put all these damn pins in this dress, anyway?" I hissed at Vic, trying to reconstruct her dress in the girl's bathroom. She had ordered it from some bootlegged website and it looked nothing like the picture, AT ALL.

"You know damn well I don't have enough tits to fill this fucker out. So, I figured—ouch! Dammit!" she screeched, after I accidentally stuck her with a safety pin in her left boob.

"My bad, shit. For somebody that ain't got no tits, you sure as hell risking deflating the little fuckers with these tacky-ass pins." I pulled and tugged for another minute or two as my

magic hands altered and hemmed that sucka, leaving not a trace of the disaster that had formerly stood before me.

"You saved my life tonight, Cash!" she yelped, grinning from ear to ear. "I swear I owe you."

"Girl please, you don't owe me. We sistas forever. There ain't nothing that could ever change that. After all, I am my sister's keeper."

My tears tapped the frame of the picture, leaving a puddle of pain in the midst of Vic's smiling face. I gathered my thoughts, placed the frame in my bag and made my exit, completely forgetting why I'd come in the first place.

Mr. De'Marco paced back and forth. I couldn't even imagine what he was feeling right now. He stood in front of Vic's casket, his head hung low. I wrapped my arms around him and planted a soft kiss on his cheek. His face felt cold, but not as cold as the look in his eyes.

I glanced at my girl. To say that she was casket sharp would be an understatement. With Mr. De'Marco beside himself with grief, I had stepped in to help him with all of the arrangements. They had managed to reconstruct her neck, so we could give her an open casket during the service. I refused to let anyone, other than our own people, coordinate Vic's final event.

We stood watch, in silence, as my beautiful sister lay peacefully in her final resting place. I'd chosen a beautiful, ornate, seven-thousand-dollar bronze casket with a light pink, completely velvet interior. Of course, Vic's small frame was adorned with one of my best, specially-made designs. Vic's devoted stylist and makeup artist, Dana, had given her the most beautiful slay—from her hair to her face.

I motioned for one of Mr. De'Marco's guys to escort him to his seat. Without a word, his eyes locked onto mine and he shook his head in disbelief.

Evelyn had insisted on learning one of Vic's favorite songs by *Lucio Quarantotto*, "Time to Say Goodbye." Natalia rocked back and forth until the floodgates eventually opened, pouring out every tear that she'd been holding back, from her mother's death until today.

I tried to maintain my own composure as I walked toward the podium to read the eulogy. Mr. De'Marco kept rocking and shaking his head at the casket, stopping periodically—almost as if he were listening to see if he heard her stirring from a deep sleep. Vic was his princess, and I couldn't begin to imagine what it was like for him to lose her. I approached him and whispered a few sincere words of comfort in his ear. "We will get through this, Papa. She'll be with us, every step of the way."

I had designated my top, most loyal, and closest girls to be Vic's pallbearers. Carrying my girl out of this church would be a difficult task, but I wouldn't have it any other way. In my eyes, this was a symbol of our sisterhood and how we'd carried one another through life, no matter the circumstances.

I finally made it to the podium, my eyes scanning the church as I cleared my throat. Vic was a breath of fresh air, and she had effortlessly impacted each and every one she'd come in contact with. That being said, the church was packed to capacity.

Just knowing that her murderer might be here amongst our presence made me cringe. There was *no way* I would let her murderer slip through my fingers. I would not only hunt them down; I would make them pay in the worst way! I pursed my lips together and closed my eyes. I pictured Vic smiling as I poured my heart out, before saying my final goodbye.

CHAPTER THIRTY-ONE

Jersey: Bye Felicia

Cash finished reading the eulogy and wrapped her arms around Mr. De'Marco. She whispered into his ear a long moment before planting a kiss on his cheek. She sat back down beside me in the pew, wearing an unyielding look across her face.

Knowing exactly what that look meant, I grabbed her hand and massaged it gently with my thumb. I could feel her body begin to relax as Evelyn sang her heart out, bringing tears to my eyes. A tear fell from Cash's face and landed on my hand. It was so cold I could've sworn it froze immediately.

"I need you to get the books from Leslie. I want to know every appointment Vic had the last forty-eight hours before her death. I want names, addresses, everything. Somebody knows something...and I'm gonna be sure to make them feel the wrath for killing my sister," she sighed.

"The last thing I need is her dad knowing what her true position in the enterprise was. I can't have him remembering his daughter that way. I want this shit done quietly. Keep her name in the clear. I'll link up with Slick and see what he can do on his end. Brains is gonna link up with Natalia's Uncle Ricardo. They're going to put a price out as a reward for her murderer's head. I just can't believe the damn hotel surveillance cameras didn't catch shit," she whispered, shaking her head.

I sat there silently. It was such a sad situation. Vic was gone way too soon. Leaving this earth so violently and so mysteriously, there was no way Vic's poor soul could rest peacefully until we found out the truth behind the circumstances that led to her death. This whole situation was messed up. *Rest assured, this shit's not gonna end pretty*, I thought.

I cleared my calendar for the rest of the week and got to work on everything Cash had requested as well as some other pressing shit I needed to tend to.

"Leslie, I need the books from last week...all of 'em," I ordered.

"All of them? That's going to take some time, Jersey. I..."

I took a deep breath and leaned in over her desk. Nearly kissing her lips, I spoke to her in a calm, solemn tone. "Okay, here's the deal. Either you have them shits on my desk in twenty minutes, or I'm gonna redecorate your entire cubical retrieving 'em myself. You choose!"

Ignoring the dour look on her face, I walked out of her office calling over my shoulder, "See you shortly, ma."

"Okay ladies, check this out. I need all of my girls doing double time this week. I have some higher priority things that I need to tend to and..."

I was holding a staff meeting with my team when my attention was diverted. I noticed one of the ladies obviously had more important shit going on. Realizing everyone's attention was now focused on her, Ebony finally pulled her face out of her phone long enough to let some smart shit emerge from her mouth.

"What? You can finish...I hear you," she snapped, smacking her lips. I stood there silently, grilling her with a long, blank stare. Ebony flipped her twenty-two-inch, Brazilian weave over her right shoulder and asked, "Damn, Jersey. You gonna stare me down the whole meeting?"

Yo, this young bitch has really been buggin' lately, dead ass. Her little attitude problem was starting to get me tight, na' mean? I don't play that disrespectful shit in my division. I'd gladly transfer her ignorant ass into Ev's or Leslie's, real talk.

Calming my nerves, I blew out a sigh of frustration and counted to five. I was really trying not to spaz out on her, especially after Cash and I had that discussion about my hot head the day I went upside Leslie's.

"You got to know when to be a lady and when to be a goon." Hearing Cash's voice in the back of my mind brought me back to rationality.

"Look Ebony, I don't have time to go back and forth with your ass today, or any other day, for that manner. We're pressed for time and I got mad shit—"

Ebony rolled her eyes and interrupted once more. "Maaann, ain't nobody trying to hear this..."

Another girl interrupted her, with an incredulous expression on her face. "Ebony, why the fuck you bein' so foul? It ain't Jersey's fault Marc turned your basic ass down the other night. That's what your thirsty ass get for trying to stick your hand in the cookie jar."

Ebony's body jerked up from her seat in a rage. "Bitch, fuck you! Find you some business and quit trying to keep tabs on mine."

I sat back and took it all in, watching the show. These hoes haven't learned shit. All that barking was a fucking waste of time and energy. They obviously wanted to perform. Otherwise, the blows and weave patches would already be flying high.

Although I must admit, hearing Marc's name still gave me a rush. It felt good to know he wasn't going, at least not with anyone else affiliated with LLE.

"You mad?" the other girl continued to taunt Ebony. "Or nah?"

Feeling a headache approaching, I intervened. "Look, stop frontin'. Neither one of you bitches wanna take it there. You broads keep fuckin' up my meeting, I'm gone beat the brakes off both you hoes, na' mean?"

I shot Ebony a "just-give-me-a-reason" scowl. She was smarter than she looked, 'cause the bitch changed tune real quick.

Sucking my teeth, I got up and moved in her direction, maintaining eye contact. "But uh, yeah, Ebony, you can collect your shit. You're dismissed until further notice. You already know—we don't break the code, dead ass."

Ebony gave a weak-ass final attempt at salvaging her job. "But—"

"Bye, Felicia," I countered, flaring my nostrils. "Meeting adjourned!"

My feelings were all over the place. I had shit coming at me from every which way. Ever since I'd dismissed the meeting, I couldn't stop thinking about Marc. I wanted to call him badly, but too many other things required my attention at the moment.

I can still hear the echo from our last argument. The words he'd spoken seemed imprinted on my heart. *"I've grown to love you, everything about you, woman. Why are you fighting us?"* I made a solemn oath to call him later that evening after I got my head straight.

I sat in my office trying to piece some things together as I shuffled through the files Leslie had plopped on my desk two minutes before the deadline. I'm guessing she'd learned that I ain't for none of her bullshit from our last encounter. I say what I mean, and I mean what I say.

On another note, this shit with Simone just didn't sit right with me. After seeing her and Leslie in that hotel, I immediately started doing some probing of my own.

I hired a private investigator to do some digging on Simone and her husband. The husband, Michael Pinelli, was getting mad *guap*. I browsed through the last report the investigator had provided. It pretty much summed everything up in a nut-shell.

Michael Pinelli was the founder of a hugely successful Fortune 500 company. He had adopted a baby boy thirteen years ago. He'd gone through a massive depression two years ago, al-most causing him to lose everything.

Overall, he was pretty typical for a rich white dude. So was his marriage. Reading aloud, I tried to finish up as quickly as possible. "No extramarital affairs...blah, blah, blah... Wait, this can't be right. What the...?"

I snatched up the phone and called Jeremy, my PI. "Hey, can you meet me tonight? Seven sharp... No, it can't wait... What do you mean, 'threats?' From who? No, wait—don't hang up...I need—"

The call disconnected. I waited a few minutes, then called him again, my hands shaking with each number I pressed. "No longer in service? Yo, this shit is eerie, son!" I said, slamming down the phone.

Gathering my things, I quickly stood. A manila envelope slipped from between one of the files I was holding. Something in my gut didn't feel right. I pushed my door closed and slowly began opening the envelope. Suddenly, a loud buzzing noise startled me. I jumped, dropping the envelope and its contents.

"Shit," I hissed. I fumbled through my things, searching for my phone. I shot Cash a quick response to her text and grabbed my bag. I bent over to pick up the envelope and noticed the contents it once held were pictures. They were now scattered all over my office floor.

They were pictures of me as a young girl in Honduras and pictures of me as a teenager in Brooklyn. I peered closer and quickly retrieved a picture that gave me the most peculiar feeling. It was a picture of Mister and the bloody aftermath of a job well done, on my end, to escape his captivity.

My heart raced as I quickly shuffled through the rest of the pictures. I collected them all, getting more and more agitated. Things were beginning to unravel, leaving me no other choice but to fast forward to my next option.

I placed the call. "Tony, it's time...no, fuck that. We gotta do this shit, now! Somebody knows something! It's 'go' time!"

CHAPTER THIRTY-TWO

Slick: Can't Keep a Real Nigga Down

"Slick, why the fuck you always gotta conveniently make your way out before daylight? You act like we ain't been fuckin' around long enough for us to spend an entire night together."

I continued pulling up my gray sweats. Then leaned in to plant a kiss on Lisa's forehead.

"So you ain't got shit to say, huh? You got a whole lot to say when you runnin' all up in this wet ass..."

Losing my cool, I stopped lacing up my wheat-colored Timbs and turned to face her nagging ass. "Lisa! Cease that shit, man!" I said, annoyed with the bullshit.

Her smooth, cocoa-brown skin glistened under the lights of the chandelier. Her bangs accentuated her pretty face and slanted eyes, making her look like a black china doll. She formed her full lips into a lusty pout. "I promise, I'll make it worth your while," she purred.

As tempting as that shit was, I opted out, pulling on my hooded sweater. "Nah, I got moves to make. Plus, yo' ass ain't got no act right. If you over there whinin' about me never stayin' over now, yo' ass really gone be a nuisance if I fuck around and spend a whole night with yo' ass. You need to invest in a hobby or some shit," I recommended.

"Boy, bye. I got hobbies. You ain't gotta stunt on me though, Slick."

Letting out a sarcastic chuckle, I stood up and began looking through the closets, under the bed, behind the curtains and shit.

"What are you looking for? You got all yo' shit over there in that lonely-ass corner," she huffed.

"Bitch, I'm looking for the fuckin' audience. 'Cause as far as I know, you and me the only ones up in this condo. The fuck I gotta stunt for?" I asked, zipping up my jacket.

"I ain't mean it like that...dang," she pouted, folding her arms.

Trying to leave on a good note, I decided to make light of my departure. I walked around the king-sized bed and leaned over, kissing her on the nape of her neck. She threw her arms around me, savoring the moment. I pulled away gently. "Be cool, ma. I gotta get to it!"

"Damn, fammo. It took you long enough. I was starting to think ya ass fell in the pussy. I was starting to worry, especially since ya ass don't know how to swim," Smoke clowned.

"Yo' ass in a joking mood today, huh? Even if I did fall in the pussy, yo' pussy-whipped ass can't save a nigga, no way. The way that Latina *mami* got ya ass wide open and shit," I countered.

Pinching his chin, Smoke got quiet on me. Then he just went back to giving his normal head nod.

"Yeah, fool. Yo' ass don't wanna see me. You know I get ya ass every time, my dude."

"Yeah? Keep talking shit. Ya ass gone *get up* out my vehicle, puss' ass," Smoke came back at me.

I burst out laughing, turning the knob to the stereo system up.

Smoke smacked my hand out the way. "Get yo' greasy-ass hands off my system."

This shit could go on for hours. Smoke's ass could never win. The shit tickled me all the time too.

"Aye, I need you to keep ya ear to the streets on what really went down with ole girl."

"Ole girl?" Smoke asked.

"Yeah, shit that went down at the telly. I was tellin' you 'bout that shit the other day. That was Cash's right hand."

Smoke took a pull from the blunt, exhaling the smoke slowly. "Yep, that was Ev's homegirl, too. She been real fucked up about that shit. I can't really comfort her ass, not for real. Shit. As many lives I done took, I became numb to that shit a long time ago. You feel me?"

I nodded, understanding him all too well. However, when it came to Cashmere, I couldn't be numb to shit that had to do with her.

Smoke pulled the car up to this shabby-ass trap house. Shooting him a quick glance, I began scoping out the surroundings. He put the car in park and gave his classic head nod, rubbing his hands together.

Already knowing the deal, I waited for him to hop out. Soon as he did, I slid into the driver's seat and cocked back my burner, ready for the unknown. With the doors wide open, I could see and hear everything that was transpiring.

"Y'all niggas ready to meet yo' maker?" He was too fucking quick. He grabbed the lady by her throat, throwing her to the ground. "Get on yo' knees, bitch," Smoke commanded, pointing the gun at the man's dome.

"Please...don't do this, sir... I have money...lots of it...in the back. Just take the money. I won't mention this again."

"Shut the fuck up," Smoke commanded viciously.

The woman tried to scamper away. Without even turning in her direction, Smoke reached back and nonchalantly blew her head off.

"Gina!" the man screamed.

Smoke's face turned cold. His evil sneer set the tone for the rest of the visit. "Ricardo sends his condolences. So sorry for your loss..."

After cleaning up the evidence, Smoke hopped in the passenger seat. I put the car in drive and gave my cousin some dap for executing that shit like a pro.

We had eliminated one more fool, bringing us closer to our ultimate motive. The woman was simply an unfortunate byproduct. It would take us no time at all to gain clout in Ricardo's circle. That power and respect would grant us full access to the city and many more rewards to come.

That nigga Brains ain't gone know what hit 'im. He was in for a rude awakening, indeed. He knew I was loyal. He also should've known this shit was gone eventually come to a halt. He had his chance to do right by me. And that shit was an epic fail.

He may not have any knowledge of my future goals, but it sure seemed like he was trying to keep me stagnant. I wasn't gonna let that nigga stop my climb to the top. What did he think I was gonna do? Give up all that blood and sweat I'd shed, putting in work all these years? Let my dreams go, to fulfill his? On some real shit, you can't keep a real nigga down but you can be used as a stepping stone on the way up!

CHAPTER THIRTY-THREE

Cash: Nothing Personal—This is Business

My best friend's death was taking an intense toll on my mental. I was ready to shake the city up, taking out anything and anybody that stepped in my way.

Mr. De'Marco was so distressed he actually started putting hits out on any muthafucka that had ever looked at him wrong. Over the past week, twenty-nine bodies were found across the West Coast. All of them, except five, were definitely hits from the Mafia.

The other deaths were just as ruthless. I wouldn't put it past Ricardo to use Vic's death to camouflage his own clatter, serving retribution for the murders of Claudia and Javier. With both the mob and the cartel out for blood, no one was safe—especially when it came to their families.

For me, there was no mistake distinguishing a hit that came from Mr. De'Marco. Growing up with Vic, I'd learned that it was vital to become skilled at other tactics, especially if I wanted to eliminate my own teacher. So, I made it my business to learn and master something other than what Brains and Slick had taught me. Brains may play that "behind-the-scenes" shit, but trust and believe, that fool's a monster when he deemed it necessary.

So, I paid close attention to the mob, and not only when I was around Vic. Hell, sometimes I'd even follow them without their knowledge that I was there, watching. I had my ways and years of practice doing these types of "magic" tricks. Most importantly, I'd learned a lot about making a name for myself while still remaining a mystery.

I needed to clear my head and put my nerves at ease. Knocking back a few drinks always seemed to do the trick. All that would have to wait though, because duty called. There was money calling, and I was certainly gonna answer.

I got dressed in a pair of white J Brand skinny jeans, and a low-cut tank. Then I slid on my white Burberry denim jacket and added a beautiful antique gold and diamond neckpiece. I decided against the .22; and instead concealed my .380 in my oversize gold Celine bag.

Although I didn't have many enemies, I still didn't trust Simone. There's always a bitch ready to take your place, even if it meant taking you out in the process. On top of that, I couldn't trust that the shit with Vic had no relation to LLE. So, I preferred to play it safe.

Me: "Aye, meet me at the drop box at 8 sharp."

Jersey: "Bet, ma...I got two stops to make and I'm there."

Me: "Bet."

The only ones that knew about this transaction—besides Simone—was Jersey and myself. Simone claimed that she needed to be as far away from the job as possible. She'd left half of the money in an underground parking garage in a 2008 silver Jetta, parked closest to the elevator.

I pulled up to the spot, parking a few cars down and shot a quick text to Brains, wishing him a safe trip. If I really gave a shit, I'd think he had another bitch on the low, as much as he'd been traveling solo lately.

Although I lightweight regretted agreeing to this meeting already, it was far too late for all that. Deep in my gut, I knew something didn't feel right about this, but my damn pride wouldn't let me turn back.

"Where the fuck is Jersey?" This had to be the fifth time I checked my watch in the past five minutes. "Fuck this shit," I mumbled to myself, exiting my car.

My shimmery gold Sophia Webster stilettos with the butterfly wing–ankle wrap echoed through the hollow parking garage. The loud click-clacks sounded off like firecrackers as I walked toward the designated vehicle. Suddenly, a feeling of discomfort nearly smothered me, but I soldiered on.

I popped open the trunk of the Jetta with the spare key Simone had given me. I lifted the spare tire and pulled an envelope out of the well. "Ain't no damn seventy-five bands in here...what the fuck is this shit?" I opened the envelope and pulled out a handwritten note...

"Your turn, ma! CASH OUT!"

The shit I was seeing didn't even set in properly until I felt a hard poke in the arch of my back.

"Bitch, don't move."

This muthafucka behind me obviously had no fucking idea who he was dealing with. If he did, he must have a death wish. I stood there silently, not uttering a single word.

"Where yo' little-ass .22 at?" the mystery person asked, patting my right leg. This muthafucka knew exactly where to look, too.

"I ain't got it," I said calmly, thinking of a strategy to get this shit cracking. "Where's the money?" I asked, nonchalantly.

"Bitch, you don't talk unless I tell you to. Money is the last thing yo' ass should be concerned about," he hissed.

"Is that right? Well then, what else sh—" Before I could finish my statement, I was struck in the back with a forceful blow, causing me to drop to my knees.

"Yo' tough ass don't listen. Do you?" The mystery person slowly strolled around to stand in front of me. It was dark as shit in the garage. The mask and hooded sweater didn't help much

either. Everything about this shit spelled out "hit." The muthafucka talked too much to come from De'Marco, and I sure as hell
ain't see that one coming no how.

I was struck again, in the face this time, by another powerful blow, causing my whole damn jaw to ripple in pain. I spat out
blood, giving him an evil glare. "You may as well kill me now.
'Cause if you don't, I'm most definitely gone come hard for yo'
pussy ass."

The pistol struck the side of my head, this time, filling me
with red-hot, excruciating pain. He stood there silently, before
raising the gun, placing it dead smack in the center of my forehead.

This can't be happening right now, I thought. He obviously
had a job to do and was dead set on getting it done. I swallowed
hard, pissed at the fact that shit was about to go down like this. I
hadn't done all this shit for nothin'. Muthafuckas had to pay for
killing my family. Things ain't supposed to happen like this. I
couldn't go out like this! My mission was compromised, the element of surprise quickly vanished. The chance for me to inflict
my long-sought retribution, now gone.

"Can I ask you one question?" I whispered.

He pushed the gun harder into my head, as if trying to leave
a brand. "What?" he growled.

I cleared my throat. "Who sent you?"

The fool began to laugh maniacally. He quickly calmed and
cocked his piece. He strengthened his grip around the .40 cal. I

closed my eyes and heard him say, "Nothing personal—this is business!"

Within seconds...shots rang out, followed by the sound of a faint heartbeat.

CHAPTER THIRTY-FOUR

Smoke: The Streets Chose Me

"**E**velyn, you gotta eat somethin', ma. You can't sit here and starve yourself forever." I sat down beside her with a bowl of chicken and rice soup. "Open yo' mouth, girl. Let me see them pretty lips wrap around this spoon."

She couldn't force her pout long enough before she smiled, flickering her eyes at a nigga. "You so damn silly," she said, finally opening her mouth.

Seeing her hurt, I tried my best to make light of the situation. I had no clue how to console her aside from being my regular, comical self. I fed her the soup like she was my seed or some shit. I didn't know what it was about this chick. She was the first in a hot minute that had me wide open.

"Yeah, that's right, baby. Suck all them juices off that muthafucka," I teased, feeding her the last bits of soup left.

"You so damn freaky, boy."

I gave her a witty smirk, placing the empty bowl on the end table. "Boy? Woman, don't you know this all man right here." I stood, taking off my wife beater. I stared down at the monster rising in my pants at the sight of her nipples imprinted on her tank.

"Oh yeah, *papi?*" she asked, raising her brows. She got up off the couch and grabbed the bowl. I watched her ass eat up her boy shorts as she pranced her sexy ass over to the kitchen sink. "Show me how a man puts it down for his woman," she commanded, turning around.

She didn't even realize I was right behind her. Ev had a look of desperation in her eyes like she needed to feel every bit of me up inside her, right now. I tailored to her pain with soft kisses along her neckline. I softly gripped her hair, tilting her head back. I planted my lips on hers, pinning her against the counter and pulling her panties off. I cupped her by her juicy ass and slowly lifted her, placing her up on the countertop.

I hadn't even realized she had already pulled down my boxers. I stepped out of them, holding her gaze as I ripped the condom wrapper open with my teeth. I slid my monster up and down her slit until I could feel her juices saturating it. I stuck the head in, for just a second. Only to feel her tight, wet pussy grab hold and squeeze the shit out of me. I gave her short strokes until her muscles gave in to the pressure. Sensing her eagerness, I backed away and rolled the rubber onto my hard dick. She pulled me back toward her and assisted by guiding my way back inside of her, not that I actually needed her help.

I filled her up with every inch of me. She took that shit like a "G," throwing that ass back. She gripped the counter and wrapped her smooth legs fluidly around my body. Keeping up with the pace, her walls pulsated, gripping my dick tight with every thrust, driving me crazy.

Unable to contain myself, I went savage in the pussy, stroking harder and deeper with every gasp, moan, and cry she let fall from those sexy-ass lips. "I...don't wann–a cum yet...babyyy!"

Ignoring her desperate plea for leniency, I gripped her around her neck. "Shut the fuck up and let that pussy cum all over this dick," I ordered.

"Awe, shit... I'm 'bout to...cum... No, baby...wai—... I...hate you... Slow..." The more she begged, the deeper I plunged, sending her ass through all sorts of orgasmic waves. I let up for a second, alternating between slow and shallow strokes with the sensual and deep strokes. She bit down on her bottom lip, letting out soft sexy moans.

I smirked at the fact that she kept losing her grip because she couldn't keep her legs from shaking. I pulled out quickly, grabbed her legs, and wrapped them around my neck. She leaned back, gripping the back of my head, and rotated her hips.

"Mmm hmmm..." she hummed and panted. Her body trembled as I licked her slit one final time, sucking out the rest of whatever juices she had left before going back in for the finale.

I eased out of her and lifted her off the counter. I cradled her in my arms, kissing her with every step, making my way over to the sofa. I set her down gently, watching her body relax and her eyes close. I covered her with a throw and eased away, giving a slight head nod before going to clean myself up for tonight's meeting.

After taking a long shower, I sat at the edge of the bed in Evelyn's room, deep in thought. My mind was on that shit Leslie sprung on me the other day. *A son...13?* I couldn't begin to think about how much of his life I'd missed.

How does he look? Can he hoop like his old man? Is he a nut case like his damn mama? How are his grades? Is he a hothead? Or, does he keep his cool, like his daddy?

My head was full of unanswered questions. On top of that, she'd just sent my little man off to be with some fuckin' strangers. I know I ain't perfect, by far. Who's to say how shit would've went had I been seventeen with two naggin' ass baby mamas? But I ain't never ran from no damn responsibility. I'd seen enough of that shit to know that ain't the man I am or ever would be.

That should've been my choice to deal with, handle, or whatever the fuck else I needed to do to make sure my kids had a daddy in their lives. Not the choice of some reckless-ass bitch and her crooked-ass cop of a daddy. Had it been up to his ass, I would've been put under the jail to spare his mental case of a daughter. His ass thought shit was sweet. I guess it was his bad for not doin' the shit properly. Leaving shit to be flushed away here and swept under the rug there, yet still effectively stripping me away from my own shitty-ass life.

"Marcus, there have been some changes with the charges against you," the public defender prick said, adjusting his crooked-ass glasses.

"What you mean, changes? Y'all figured out that I was telling the truth the whole time?" I asked, leaning into the glass window with a vicious mug on my face.

"Well, uh...not exactly. You see, there have been some discrepancies..."

Becoming annoyed, I interrupted his stuttering Stanley-ass. "Man, quit tap dancing around and spit that shit out."

He shuffled around some papers and started reading some shit that may as well have been another language, 'cause I damn sure didn't speak attorney. "What the fuck is yo' quirky ass talkin' 'bout, dude?"

He stopped reading and peered over his glasses at me. "Well, there have been some legality issues, Marcus."

I stroked my chin before leaning back and crossing my arms, speaking as calmly as possible. "What did you just say?" I asked, narrowing my eyes. Before he could answer my question, I answered it myself. "So, what you sayin' is...somebody fucked up," I smirked.

"Well...uh..." Seeing the ugly expression forming on my face, he just answered the question. "Yeah, that's about right. Somebody fucked up."

I bounced out of my seat. "Hell yeah! That mean a brotha' goin' the fuck home!" Discerning the unenthusiastic look spread across his face, I sat back down and leaned in.

"I am goin' home, right? I mean, I been in here for three months. I ain't even get to go to my own damn mama funeral. I can't get no fuckin' visitors besides my cousin and my aunt. All my damn family in Chicago. All the fuck I was doin', was visiting this shit hole–ass city. Every summer, since I was ten, my moms wanted to keep me outta trouble. So she sent me here for my high school term. Now I'm getting framed, even though the paperwork clearly states that something is fishy, fucked up, or outta' whack... Y'all still gone hold me? This corrupt-ass system ain't shit!"

The attorney took a deep breath. "Listen, we have an offer. Since you have no money, you may want to consider all of the options before taking this any further. The state doesn't want this to go public, bringing heat on the department. They are going to let you off, per se."

"Per se? The fuck you mean 'per se?'" I asked, in a pessimistic tone.

"The state's not going to let you off scot free. They have the power to make this case go away, for good, if it's kept quiet.

They need to send you off on an assignment. The task involves the military. They will pay you and train you to shoot, kill, and protect. This contract they have for you is not an easy task, but if you can make it out—completing the task successfully—you go free, financially set for life."

I gave a contemplative head nod, sealing the deal. I was just ready to get this shit over with!

I'd been cutthroat since I was eight years old, navigating my way through Chicago's city streets. After my father was murdered in cold blood, I was quickly recruited by the neighborhood hittas on Chicago's West Side. It was either kill or be killed. I damn sure wasn't on a suicide mission. To be frank, I ain't choose the streets, the streets chose me! The mission at hand was just one more war zone I had to escape from.

Beep–Beeep–Beeeep!

Slick pulled up, sounding like he was leaning on his earsplitting, loud-ass horn. He damn near tried to wake up the whole block.

"Let's go, cuzzo! We gotta bounce!" he hollered over the brash, booming music blaring from his speakers.

I grabbed my shit and gave Evelyn a soft peck on her forehead, closing the door behind me.

CHAPTER THIRTY FIVE

Slick: When Thugs Cry

"I know yo' ass saw me calling ya phone too, nigga." Smoke pulled his phone out his pocket. "Damn, my shit been on silent the whole time. My bad."

I quick-glanced over at him and realized something wasn't right about him today. I gave him a long, blank-ass stare until his ass got annoyed enough to say some slick shit.

"Damn, nigga. You wanna kiss or some shit? The fuck yo' 'honey drop' lookin' ass starin' at?" he asked, in a sarcastic tone.

"That shit right there," I said, pointing at his half-ass smirk. "Nigga, I know that Latina chick ain't got yo' bean head–ass over there, head over heels and shit."

Smoke raised an eyebrow. His face now expressionless, he sucked his teeth. "Stay the fuck out my business, Rashad."

My face turned serious, but I was still in comedy mode. "Man don't be callin' out my government name, ole scrooge face-ass nigga." We both chuckled as Smoke finished rolling up.

"Man don't be licking that shit like that. Yo' ass ain't lick enough before you came out the house?" I scoffed, feigning disgust.

Smoke turned his nose up like he was offended or some shit. "I swear to God, you make that fucked up–ass face again, I'm gone shoot yo' ass off pure reflex. Ol' retard-ass nigga. Just keep yo' fuckin' eyes on the road for the rest of the night. 'Fore you fuck around and get us both killed. Lookin' like a big-ass Bearilla with dreads."

I turned into the mansion's long driveway, bypassing all the guards this time. By now, they were pretty damn familiar with both of us. Coming soon, "familiar" would be an understatement.

"Welcome back," the girl said, guiding us into the den.

"Fellas, glad to have you back. Don't just stand there, come...sit." Ricardo motioned for us to join him.

At this point there was no need to stand anymore. We had earned our seats at the table. So we accepted the invitation without hesitation. We sat there in silence a few minutes. Suddenly, I became a little too distracted when a new guest stepped into the room.

Her exotic look reminded me of someone I had seen before, but I couldn't quite put my finger on who or where. Her sandy brown hair was pulled up into a messy bun, with bangs that complimented her hazel eyes perfectly. The *Pink* sweat suit accentuated her flat stomach and fat ass. She was definitely fuckable.

"Ahh...Natalia. I'm so glad you could join us."

Natalia? I know that name from somewhere, I thought, wracking my brain to figure this shit out.

"*Ay*, Uncle Ricardo, I was just swinging by to check on you."

Uncle? Natalia? Claudia's daughter? One of Cash's girls! Damn, how the fuck did I miss that shit?

I watched her as she took a seat across from me. They chatted briefly before she excused herself, extending her apologies for interrupting our meeting. I could tell she knew exactly who I was, just as I did her, now. We locked gazes a final time before she shot me a sly wink and disappeared.

"Now, fellas...let's talk business."

I thought that meeting was never gonna end. I damn near started to fake a seizure or some shit, just to get the fuck out of there. Lisa's ass was blowing up my phone so bad my damn battery died. I was lightweight glad to finally get some peace from her dramatic ass.

Ring...ring...ring...ring...ring...

Finally done with the meeting and back in the car, Smoke answered his phone. "Yeah...what you want with him?"

I cut my eyes at the nigga, knowing damn well Lisa bet not be on that phone. This bitch would have to be the feds or some shit to pull that one off.

"Evelyn, slow down. I can't understand you when you starting speaking that shit, girl! Cash?"

Seeing the confusion etched on his face, mixed with hearing Cash's name thrown in the mix, caused me to snatch the phone from his ear. "Yo, what up with Cash, ma?"

Her Spanish accent was thicker than I remembered, but I tried to follow. "I got a call from the hospital, they found my card in her wallet, and..."

I pulled the damn car over so I could think straight. "Hospital? What you talkin' about?"

"I need you to see if you can reach Brains. I don't know his number, and I can't reach anyone else. I'm at the hospital right now. Please call him and have him get here, asap. Cash was shot!"

The call disconnected and my head instantly started spinning in circles. "Fuck that nigga Brains. We on our way, now!"

Smoke ain't ask no questions, he just went along for the ride. It fucked me up when I felt a single tear trickle down my face. I didn't even bother wiping it off. Just know you done hit a nerve if you got me shedding a tear... I'm human and all, but yo' ass betta' know, it's real when thugs like me cry!

CHAPTER THIRTY-SIX

Cash: Even the Devil Was Once an Angel

I woke up disoriented, hearing faint beeping noises and chatter projecting from out in the hallway. "Hey, baby. What the hell happened to you?" The sound of Evelyn's voice made me wonder what the hell was going on.

I couldn't think straight right now. The pain in my head and arm were getting worse. The gauze pad on my shoulder appeared to be soaked with blood. All I could remember was the sound of a gun going off. I didn't even know how the hell I got here.

"Daphne here is lucky to be alive," a deep voice rang out. Evelyn's confused expression caused me to turn my head to my left to get a better look.

"Mr. Mike? What are you doing here? What are you talking about?" My voice was hoarse and raspy.

Mike, Simone's husband, stood up and walked over to my bedside, handing me a cup of water. "Well, you almost got yourself killed, young lady. I caught the man just in time." He patted my shoulder reassuringly, giving me a genuine smile of endearment. "I was walking to my car and saw you on the ground, staring down the barrel of a gun. I drew my own gun immediately and discharged it. Thankfully, this happened just in time for his shot to miss your head and hit you in the shoulder instead. My shot killed him instantly," he relayed.

"You were in and out of consciousness. I held you up until the police and ambulance arrived. You lost a lot of blood, but they were able to successfully remove the bullet. You definitely have a concussion though."

Feeling the bandage around my head, I couldn't believe what had happened. I was thankful to be alive, but enraged to be in this mess at the same damn time.

Mike, wisely discerning that I could use some time to process the influx of information, patted my shoulder reassuringly. "I'll be in the waiting area. I need to get Marcus a bite to eat. I'm sure you two want some privacy," he smiled, excusing himself.

I managed to return the gesture with a thin, but grateful, smile. I grabbed his hand, gripping it as tightly as I could. "Thank you, Mike," I told him sincerely.

"Anytime, Daphne," he responded, before disappearing out the door and around the corner.

"Girl...who the hell is that? And, why does he keep calling you 'Daphne?'" Evelyn questioned cynically, with her nose all scrunched up. "What the fuck is going on here?" She threw her hands up in frustration.

I let out a deep sigh. After a moment of silence, Evelyn loudly smacked her lips, placing her hands on her hips. She impatiently waited for a logical explanation behind all of this.

I just gave her a blank stare. Hell, I was trying to figure all this shit out, too. I could feel aches and pains all up and through my body. But my heart ached more than my body and my head. I was in a messed up, vulnerable position. That wasn't cool!

The only thing I could do was let out another sigh of frustration. I couldn't even shake my head, it hurt so bad. I adjusted my body to the best of my ability and prepared to break this down to Ev in the raw.

"Daaammn, *mami!*" That was all Evelyn could say after I gave her the rundown on everything that had happened, from the moment Simone approached me with the proposition until today.

"So, you don't think Simone's crazy ass could've conjured this shit up? I definitely can't see Jersey doin' this foul shit, Cash!"

I rolled my eyes, contemplating her analysis of the situation. The thought of Jersey doing this shit made my whole body pulse with hurt. Ev moved up to my bedside.

"I did reach out to her, though. Her damn phone went straight to voicemail," she said, twisting her lips and waving off the implications. "I managed to get in contact with Slick. I was trying to tell him to call Brains when my battery died," she continued, smacking her lips in frustration.

The sound of Slick's name made my heart race. He would be here before Brains' ass. I'm sure of that.

"Knock, knock," the doctor chirped and stepped in, wearing a pleasant smile. "How are you feeling, Daphne?"

I didn't even bother correcting her—maybe it was better this way. "A little sore, but I'll manage."

"Well, I have some 'good' news and some 'not-so-good' news. Which would you like first?"

I gave her an incredulous look, as if to say, *could the shit get any worse*? "News is news, right?" I responded, pushing myself to sit up taller, ready for her to get to the point.

She glanced over at Ev, then back at me.

"She can stay," I told her, reading her concern.

"Well, Ms..." Nothing this woman said even registered in my mental. My mind drifted and suddenly filled with thoughts of Meredith, Vic, and Jersey. I heard my mama's voice. It seemed like it was blaring through the walls.

"*In these streets—hell, in life—you can't trust no one, Cashmere. Even the damn devil was once an angel.*"

"Ma'am, do you have any questions?" the doctor asked.

Not even knowing what the hell she'd just said, I managed to shake my head. I hadn't even noticed her moving closer to my bedside. I sure didn't feel her checking my blood pressure.

"Well, there you have it. I ordered a few more routine tests. If everything comes back okay, you will likely be discharged in a couple of days." She completed my vitals check. Then she excused herself from the room.

Before I could open my mouth, the door opened once again, revealing the face of the man that made my heart smile.

"If this yo' way of taking a break, shit's not approved, by any means," Slick joked, planting a sincere kiss on my forehead.

"Yo' ass always gotta find some humor in the silver lining," I fussed back at him.

"Nah, ain't a bit of humor in that funk breath you blowin' over here," he chuckled, stroking my left cheek.

The look in his eyes was one I'd never seen before, a look of sincerity and affection. He glanced over at Ev. I already knew what time it was. "Ev, can you excuse us for a moment?"

She had this weird glow on her face. "No problem, *mami*. I'll be in the waiting room..." She gave Slick a hesitant, awkward gaze.

"Yeah, man. He out there, damn," he chuckled.

Confused as the day before me, I asked, "What was that about?"

He waved his hand, dismissively. "Fuck all that..." His face suddenly turned deathly serious, and a look I was all too familiar with resurfaced. "What the hell happened to you, Cash?"

I let out a final exasperated breath, rolling my eyes to the back of my head. Then I stared into Slick's eyes with cold, callous thoughts of retaliation. "I'm still tryin' to find that shit out. But, please believe, somebody knows something!"

CHAPTER THIRTY-SEVEN

Smoke: Safe with Me

I'd been so busy chillin' with Ev and Slick, I hadn't even had a chance to find out if Leslie was able to get me the connect to my boy. I pulled out the card she'd given me and dialed the number. The phone rang once and went straight to voicemail.

I attempted to hit her up one last time when out of the corner of my eye I caught Ev approaching. She called herself sneaking up on a brotha. "What up, ma!" I called, spoiling the fun.

"Damn, Smokey. You always gotta—"

Before she could finish, I grabbed her arm and pulled her close to me. "Hush that noise and gimme a kiss, woman."

She cut her eyes at me but did as she was told. Then she walked around in front of me and sat on my lap, wrapping her arms around my neck.

I could tell she had a lot on her plate. Having one friend mysteriously murked and another in a hospital bed after nearly getting murked was a lot for anyone to bear.

"How's Cash?" I asked, stroking her hair between planting soft kisses on her forehead.

"She's holding up...I just...shit's not adding up, and I don't know what the hell this shit is about... Am I next?"

I grabbed her shoulders firmly, pushing her back to see her face. "Ain't shit gone happen to you. Ya' ass betta' know that," I assured her.

She leaned back into me, laying her head on my chest. I held her body just enough to give her a sense of security. It took her no time to fall asleep in my arms.

"Over there, Marcus."

The sound of my name caught me off-guard. *Who the fuck would be calling me by my government in this damn hospital?* I thought, scanning the room.

The only people in the room, besides the secretary, me and Ev, was a white dude reading a magazine and a boy surfing through the vending machine, babysitting a basketball under his right arm. Just as I began to write the voice off to coincidence and my heightened sense of paranoia, the boy turned, facing my direction. He looked like someone I'd seen before. I stared him down for a second, trying to figure this shit out, until Slick suddenly emerged from around the corner, motioning me over.

Hating to disturb babygirl, I gently patted her leg. "Baby, lemme go holla at Slick real quick."

She smoothed out the frizz in her hair and stood to her feet. "Ok, baby. I'm gonna go check on Cash."

"Cool."

She kissed me softly on the lips. "Thank you for making me feel safe," she whispered before drifting off to aide her homegirl.

"Oh, baby. Thank you for keeping me safe," Slick mocked, trying to sound like a female and irritating the hell out of me.

"Man, shut yo' goof ass up," I snapped back, slapping his dreads. "You ready, my nigga?"

"Nah, man. I ain't leavin' her here, Smoke," he answered, with narrowed eyes. "This was a hit, and I ain't gone leave her alone 'til I find out what the fuck is goin' on."

I knew how he felt about shorty, no matter how much he denied that shit. One thing's for sure, cuzzo was ready to put in work.

"I need you to get ahold of Ricardo. We gone have to miss that meeting, cuz. Break this shit down as clearly as possible. We've put in more than enough work for him to know we ain't on no shady shit."

I gave him a head nod, not even bothering to argue about his decision. The last thing I wanted to do was leave Evelyn's life at stake, especially after I gave her my word. Missing the meeting was risky, but like Slick said, we'd put in enough work for him to know what it was.

I stepped outside the hospital to make a few calls. A bouncing basketball came hurtling my way, damn near knocking my phone out of my hand. Catching it with my other hand, I turned to the little homie and nodded.

"This you?" I asked.

"Yes sir," he answered, looking me in the eyes.

"You like to ball, lil' homie?" I asked.

"Yes, sir."

"You any good?"

He just shrugged his shoulders. "I guess. I'm alright."

Something about little homie was all too familiar... "How old are you?"

"Thirteen. What's up with all the questions? You the police or something?"

I chuckled, amused at his comment. "Nah, I'm just making small talk," I responded, throwing the ball back to him.

Catching the ball, he nodded. "Thanks, mister."

I nodded back. He turned to walk away, but something inside of me said to stop him. "Ay, lil' homie...what's ya' name?" I asked.

Preparing to enter back through the sliding doors, he stopped momentarily. He dribbled the ball one last time before walking through the doors. "Marcus," he called back.

His response caused my whole body to shift into a coma-like trance as I watched him disappear into thin air.

CHAPTER THIRTY-EIGHT

Slick: Get Ready for a Long Ride

This was the day Smoke and I were supposed to make our final rounds, pick up money, and make this last hit down at the warehouse with Ricardo. We had already done the bulk of the work on our own. We had all the drugs moved to the warehouse just in time for the meeting with a new connect out of Dallas.

We left our trademark in the worst way, yet still managed to remain untraceable in the process. I glanced at my watch, noting it was 6:45 p.m. I sat next to Cash's hospital bed, reading *The 48 Laws of Power* on my phone and patiently waiting for the call telling us that shit was in the clear.

I gazed lovingly at Cash as she rested peacefully. My phone's vibration indicated I had a text coming through. It was Brains checking in. I put my phone back in my pocket, not even bothering to respond.

Then, I glanced up at the television and damn near choked. I immediately rushed toward the waiting room to find Smoke and tell him to turn to the news channel.

He fumbled through the channels until I snatched the damn remote, forgetting he hadn't been here in a hot minute. I turned to the news myself, surprised to see that nigga, Ricardo, being escorted out of the warehouse in handcuffs.

"Turn that shit up," Smoke said, his eyes glued to the television.

> "After years of investigation, more than fifteen thousand pounds of cocaine and over eighty million dollars in cash and firearms were seized this afternoon as combined efforts of the FBI, DEA, and ATF executed search warrants on a North Side warehouse here in Los Angeles. Federal authorities agree that this may be one of the largest drug busts in history on US soil. Among those detained was drug lord Ricardo Escalante of the Laredo cartel, one of the largest spread across North and South America. Authorities believe drugs and money seized today will cripple the Laredo cartel. Escalante has been a Most Wanted figure in the ongoing investigation, brought to closure today."

I sat there in disbelief, letting the shit simmer. All sorts of shit was running through my head. One thing in particular was the fact that only half the drugs and money was reported to have been confiscated in the bust. Either they kept it for themselves, or Smoke and I had done a hell of a job stashing the shit for security purposes. The shit that went down with Cash was fucked up, but it definitely prevented us from being in the wrong place at the wrong time.

"I gave Evelyn some cash to get you a few items while you're here. I had Natalia set the room up just how you like it, and we got enough snacks and shit..."

Cash was looking around, all wide-eyed and amazed. "Damn, Rashad. You livin' nice! Which one of your floozies helped you decorate, is all I wanna know? 'Cause I know you didn't do it by yourself," she said, raising her eyebrow and pressing her sexy lips together.

"There you go, callin' out my damn government name. You lucky you still healing," I warned over my shoulder, walking into the kitchen. "You want some–thing?" Feeling a light brush across my arm, before I could even get the words all the way out my mouth, Cash was standing next to me.

"How the hell yo' sneaky ass always manage to do that shit, girl?"

She chuckled, grabbing a handful of my hair. "It's magic," she purred, staring out the window twirling her fingers through my dreads as if pretending to retwist them one by one.

I couldn't help noticing how much damage had been done to her beautiful face. Although she was healing up rather well, it angered me to see her hurt like this.

She leaned her head onto my arm. I reached around her, pulling her into my chest like I used to do when she was a shorty. This time it felt different. I knew today she stood as a woman before me.

"Thank you for being here for me," she whispered, gazing up into my eyes, her hands roaming my body. It's like she knew exactly what to do to make me feel good. "Where's your little chicken head girlfriend at?" she continued, still whispering.

"I ain't got no girl." She tugged my shirt gently, indicating she wanted me to lean into her. "You tryin' to get yo' self in trouble, girl?" I asked, leaning in and cupping her ass, pulling her into me. Before she could answer, I did something I'd been wanting to do to her for years. I kissed her with so much passion, like I had never kissed any other chick.

Her hand moved to the back of my head, pulling me in deeper. I carefully lifted her body and carried her into the room I had set up for her. Taking care to be gentle, I placed her cautiously down on the bed as our eyes remained locked onto one another.

"You sure you wanna do this?" I asked, sliding my hands up under her shirt, invading every bit of space her bra left bare.

She bit her bottom lip and slowly nodded her head up and down, her body tensing up as she stared at me. Her eyes were filled with yearning. I had never seen her look so beautiful or vulnerable. The shit turned me on. It exposed a very intimate side of her after letting all that tough shit fly out the window.

"I just want you to take the wheel, baby," she said softly, leaning back in complete submission.

I smiled as my lips travelled to her ear. "I got you, ma. Just get ready for a long ride."

CHAPTER THIRTY-NINE

Cash: No Place I'd Rather Be

My body ached, but I wouldn't stop him if my life depended on it. Nothing else mattered at that point. I needed one moment in the midst of chaos where I didn't feel the desire to take control.

I trusted Slick with every fiber of my being. That's not something I ever remembered doing with anyone, since Meredith. He filled me up in every way imaginable, touching parts of my insides I didn't even know existed. Tonight, he became the musician, and I, his instrument. We complimented one another, becoming our own melodic band.

He plucked every string on my guitar with rhythmic strokes. He pressed every key on my piano. When he deemed it necessary, he even beat my drum, tapping into every single part of me. He had me singing soprano, alto, and his ass chimed in with the bass. When he wrapped his juicy lips around my flute, I grabbed his head and ran my fingers through his dreads.

He made sure to tend to my every desire. He knew exactly what to do to make me forget about everything but the erotic symphony he played on my body as I released a sweet, sensual song of pleasure into his ear. I deserved this. I needed him, and tonight, there was no other place I'd rather be.

"LLE, how may I help you?" Being back at work was not my ideal method to gain my strength back, but shit had to get done. It had been a week and still no one had heard from Jersey. Things were beginning to look more and more like a setup, by the day. All I wanted to know was, who she was working with? And what the fuck they stood to gain from having me dead? All for a measly seventy-five bands? Yeah, the shit still wasn't adding up.

"Yes, I hear you, sir. I'm taking it all in. I just want to be sure I send you the right girl for the job. Me? Oh no, sir...I don't work in any department that fits *your* expectations. In all actuality...I exceed them."

I took a few more calls and assessed every book from Leslie's office. Although I had my own accountant, I made sure I kept tabs on everything. If these hoes even think they can get one up on you, surely they'll try their best to slip one through the cracks.

Jersey had apparently managed to slip through. That shit made me feel so weak. Weak shit, however, don't run through my bloodline.

Ring...ring...

"LLE..."

"Cashmere? It's Judy."

"Aunt Judy? How did you get this number?"

"Neva mind that, chile. We got bigger fish to fry."

"We? The fuck you mean 'we?'"

"Look girl, I need you to meet me somewhere...I have some important information you need to know."

"Tell me now, Judy. I ain't got time for games, too much shit to do."

"I...in...two...at..."

"Judy? You're breaking up... I can't hear you... Hello?"

Click.

The call ended abruptly and I waved my hand, quickly dismissing what the hell had just transpired.

I shuffled through the rest of the books, then cleared my calendar for the rest of the day. I remembered, as an afterthought, to check on the books for the boutique as well. Satisfied with my profits, I closed the books and wrote myself a reminder memo to send out an ad for two new girls first thing tomorrow morning. Business still had to go on and one monkey sure as hell don't stop no show, especially at LLE. However, I knew that together with my best girls, we were a lethal combination.

Later that evening, Evelyn and I met at the boutique. I sifted through the inventory, checking in on my new designs.

"Cash, here's the rest of your things from the hospital. They acted like they almost didn't wanna give 'em to me, seeing how your ass jetted up out of there, refusing to cooperate." Evelyn was stuck lagging behind as Slick and I made a hasty exit, narrowly avoiding the police and their weak-ass investigative procedures.

"I'm sorry, Ev. You know how I feel about police, girl," I reminded her, scrolling through all fifty-five text messages, twenty-two missed calls, and twelve voicemails.

"*Si, mami.* I know...I know. But they're not so bad, Cash. Having a dad that's a defense attorney, I've learned a few tricks myself," she said matter-of-factly.

Yeah, I'm sure," I giggled, still clearing miscellaneous messages out of my cell phone. "Ev? I've got some things I need you to take care of for me. I'm gonna take a couple of days off, to try and figure things out. I need you to hold down the fort. Can you do that?"

Evelyn thought about it momentarily before agreeing to my request. Then, she nodded after taking everything in. I gave her the spare key to the office as well as detailed instructions, before parting ways.

It wasn't until I responded back to Slick's text, confirming tonight's rendezvous, that I noticed a voicemail message, from Vic. It was left the day she was murdered. I couldn't help but think about how things might have gone down differently, had I answered her call. I clicked the prompt to listen to the message, but the buzzing of an incoming call kicked me out of the voicemail.

"Hello."

"You have a collect call from..."

Beep...beep...

The sound of the low battery causing my cell to power down was the last thing I needed, right now. "I knew I should've got this phone checked out. Can't get shit done with a dead-ass phone," I sighed, throwing it into my bag before walking into the coffee shop. I ordered a drink, slid on my shades, and set the drink on the table. I slid into the booth right next to the person I needed to see.

"Before you try to make a scene, or even breathe wrong," I warned her, "a bullet will rip into you with no hesitation. I've been dying to test out this silencer."

The woman swallowed hard. Staring straight ahead, she gave me a slow nod.

"Good. Now that we got that clear, I have one question...where the fuck is my money?"

CHAPTER FORTY

Cash: No Fucks Given

"**C**ash..." Simone gasped my name in a breathless whisper, looking like she'd just seen a ghost.

"Nuh uh, bitch. Need I remind you of how many fucks I *don't* have to give you right now?" I lowered my voice to an angry hiss. "You put my life in jeopardy. There's no turning back from that."

She swallowed hard, closing her eyes. "I swear, I had nothing to do with that. That was not part of the plan."

"The plan? Oh, so you had a plan, huh?" I asked, with a disdainful glare.

"Look, it was all Leslie's idea."

That's the thing I hated about these white hoes. They always had shit figured out until they got caught. Then they were quick to throw someone else under the bus to spare their own ass.

"Bitch, I don't need you to tell me whose idea it was. Did you think I wasn't gonna find out about the two of you?"

Two days before...

Knock. Knock.

"Daphne? What are you doing here?"

I strolled into the immaculate office space, quickly scanning it with my eyes and temporarily tuning him out. Finally, my eyes travelled over in his direction. I noted he was now standing, casually taking a sip from his coffee mug.

My head inadvertently tilted to the side as that bizarre feeling of familiarity rushed through me. Jolting me out of my trance, he repeated his question.

"Well, what brings you here? Is everything okay? Do the police need more information? I told them everything..."

I put my hand up to stop his rambling. "I just wanted to say thank you," I told him. "Very nice office you have here," I continued, walking around the quaint space, examining his plaques, awards, and so forth. I spotted a picture on his desk and slowly picked it up. "Is one of these lovely ladies your wife?"

His hesitant smile appeared forced. "Yes...this one, right here," he confirmed, pointing at Simone.

I nodded and pointed to the right of her on the picture. "The other?" I asked, raising an eyebrow.

"Oh...that's her good friend, Leslie. Those two are inseparable," he chuckled, walking toward his desk. "Enough about me. How are you?"

"Oh, I'm doing much better now," I replied, with a look of satisfaction on my face.

After the worthwhile meeting with Mike, I tracked down Miss Leslie. And guess who was pulling up right behind her? Simone's grimy ass!

I managed to slip into the back of the building and follow them to the small dining area where they worked so hard to remain incognito. Leslie kept looking over her shoulders, paranoid. Neither of their dumb asses noticed me at the table behind them, pretending to read the newspaper.

"What do you mean 'you can't do this anymore,' Leslie?" Simone leaned in toward her, sporting a look of disbelief or confusion.

"It's complex, Simone. I don't have the time to explain in detail. Just understand that our time with one another has come to an end."

Simone banged her hands down onto the table, clearly upset. "After thirteen years of waiting, and taking in your son with the understanding that..."

Her words were drowned out as I began fitting pieces of the puzzle together in my head. The meeting, the proposition, everything was making sense now. Some things still weren't adding up, but one thing was clear...killing me was never part of the *plan for Simone. My death would serve her no purpose. Things just intertwined that way, leaving me in the mix of it all.*

Leslie showed no emotion. That bitch was grimy as fuck. Apparently, she thought she had it all figured out. Unfortunately for her, she had the shit all wrong. And her narrow-minded, shallow mindset would soon be the reason for her demise.

"We were going to take Marcus and start over. I never intended for things to go down like this... We needed Mike out of the picture. We didn't know you were going to get robbed in the process. I will pay you... Just don't..."

Simone was really good at playing the damsel in distress role. She was no victim, but I'd play along. I eased my way out of the booth, directing her toward a secluded back corner and walking behind her. I wrapped my hand around Simone's shoulders, pulling her in toward me as if giving her a relaxing massage. I used my other hand to stroke her face, as if offering some gesture of solace.

"Shhh...I know, Simone. I know. Unfortunately, you fucked with the wrong bitch." I grimaced, leaning into her body to gain leverage. Then, with maximum force, quickly twisted her neck upwards and then sideways in one swift motion, causing her body to immediately go limp.

I told y'all, I've learned from the best. I knew just how to put her to sleep, eternally, without breaking a single nail.

I propped her head against the window, as if in a sleeping position. Then I retrieved my belongings as well as hers. I left quietly, with no trace of my presence.

Twisting the life out of Simone definitely put more strain than I'd like to admit on my wounds. I swallowed three codeine tablets, washing them down with my drink, one-by-one. Slowly, I began to feel better in both body and mind as I gulped down the last of it. I shot Leslie a text from Simone's phone while waiting for mine to finish charging.

> *Simone: "Leslie can you meet tonight at 6? It won't take long. I promise. I just need to see you one last time...closure."*
>
> *Leslie: "I understand Simone. Let's try for 6:15 at the Mondrian. Room 305."*

Half an hour later, I retrieved my own phone off the charging station.

> *Me: "Did you get the address and the instructions from Ev?"*
>
> *Natalia: "I did. Clean up at 6:30. Room 305."*

I sat in my car, leaning back in my leather seat, preparing to listen to the message from Vic. I tapped the screen anxiously, not wanting to face what was enclosed in the message due to my own guilty conscience. *Fuck it.* I closed my eyes as a tear trickled down my face and pressed play.

"You have one new message."

The rustling and bustling on the other end confirmed that Vic had no idea she had even dialed my number. Chuckling silently, I shook my head and thought to myself, *I told her to put a lock on that damn phone. Somehow she always managed to butt-dial me.*

I decided to listen to the whole message, just as I would have if she had been here with her signature twisted frown. "*You don't have to be so damn nosey, Cash,*" she would always say.

"*Well, your ass obviously wants me to know what you got going on. I'll be damned if I'm gonna disappoint that juicy thang,*" I'd counter.

I was still listening to the voice message when fresh anger suddenly resurfaced, mixed with a bout of anxiety as an all too familiar voice rang out. I listened in revulsion. It was like I was standing in the room next to Vic, but bound from doing anything to stop what was taking place.

I sat there in agony as I listened to my best friend and sister's murder. Just to find out she was put to death by the same twisted bastard that murdered Meredith...

"No fucks given" was an understatement, right now. My scorecard was fully loaded and the settling of scores were at an all-time high.

CHAPTER FORTY-ONE

Brains: Anything Goes

I had too damn much on my plate at the moment. After Ricardo's arrest, I received word that he had already chosen a new connect, some Chicago boy and his cousin. I reached out to Slick, but his ass had the nerve to tell me his services were no longer available. Fuck kinda shit is that? He was really testing my mettle. To be quite honest, he might be next on my list.

Although I had a few other customers out here on the West Coast already, shit wasn't moving like I needed it to. On top of that, I had two murders on my hands that were connected to the same cartel I needed on my team to move my product.

This laying low shit wasn't helping. It actually made things worse, but I had a plan. The murders, the setup—all moves I deemed necessary to get where I needed to be. I quickly forgot their names, but they were all trying to hinder my climb to the top. So, what was I supposed to do? Give up all I'd worked for? Give up the power I'd earned? Nah, that's not gone happen.

Allowing my dreams to get deferred or go unfulfilled would be a disservice to the platform I had built for myself. Fuck all of those mediocre muthafuckas that made the mistake of getting in my way. All I had to do, was get through this small mishap and things would begin to move and shake like I needed them to. At this point, it was simple: anything goes!

"Leslie, I'm proud of you. You really proved me wrong during this process."

Leslie smiled proudly. "I told you, anything for you." She walked over to me with my drink in hand and planted a kiss on my right cheek.

"Did you manage to retrieve all the hotel footage?" I asked her, following up on the gruesome fatal fight with Victoria.

"I did. And so far, they have no leads, no person of interest," Leslie said. "I went to visit my father today, too," she continued, speaking softly in my ear, massaging the tension out of my shoulders.

I closed my eyes, stretching my neck in a circular rotation. "Yeah? How'd that work out for you?" I asked.

"Well, I chatted a bit with the clerk. After an easy five minutes, she was singing like a canary. From the looks of things, Ricardo is going away for a long time. Now that we have that out of the way, I'm sure we can focus on becoming..."

"Be–com–ing what?" I questioned, my voice going lower every syllable.

"Well, I thought after everything...we could..."

Leslie was beating around the bush, but I knew exactly what her ass was trying to get at. I took a deep breath and stood up. Then sat my drink on the table before turning to face her. "You can't be that stupid," I chuckled, stroking my goatee in amusement.

Leslie stared at me with an incredulous expression, as if in disbelief. We locked eyes and she folded her arms. "Stupid? Elaborate for me, Brian," she glared, shooting daggers my way.

"I'm just saying, you did good, Les—real good, to say the least—but that don't earn you a promotion on my team. I mean, the most you gone get outta brotha is some dope dick, or somethin' like that. Now, I can fuck you right... You deserve that much," I told her, groping myself teasingly. Leslie was furious when I said that.

I'm thinking, *she couldn't have possibly thought I would actually consider trading Cash for her wannabe, dingy ass. Leslie was fine, don't get me wrong, but she couldn't hold a candle to my baby.*

Every time I saw Cash's face it put a smile on mine. She just had it like that. Soaking up her beauty, intellect, and sense of humor just made you realize she was beautiful, on so many levels. It's rare to find a bitch you wanna be around all day, every damn day, but one that's BAD, too?! Everywhere she went every thug, white muthafucka, Latino, Asian, all of 'em...she leave muthafuckin puddles in her wake, men and women. Oh, the bitches love her too, believe dat!

I can honestly say, her and her mama definitely shared that. They were both lovable, magnetic women that could make you feel like the only other person in the room, with 'em. You couldn't see or hear shit around 'em, even surrounded by other beautiful bitches. They dominated your senses.

They both shared that natural quality and they both had that A1 pussy, too. That type of pussy that would have you sim-pin', buying bitches cars and houses. You just wanna give 'em the world. If you can't, you rather murk her ass, before lettin' another muthafucka give it to her. She definitely got it from her mama. Leslie got shit fucked up if she think she can compete with that. That's like tossing away a sack of big bills, for pocket change!

Leslie stood there for a moment, enraged, probably contemplating killing my black ass or some shit, but that didn't concern me, one bit. I raised my eyebrows and sucked my teeth. "You gone stand there and stare at me all damn day? Or you gone come finish yo' job? I got other shit I need to tend to."

She rolled her eyes and let out a long, drawn-out sigh before grabbing a cigarette from the box. "Oh? What would those things entail?" she asked, real snippy-like, knowing damn well she ain't have no business questioning me.

Annoyed, I gave her prying ass exactly what she was looking for. I walked up to her, cupped the cuff of her ass and pulled her into me. I put my other arm around her, securing the hold. I brought my lips to her earlobes and blew a soft gust of air, sending chills through her body and making her tremble. Then, I passionately whispered in her ear, "Bitch, I'm goin' home to my woman. Yo' services are no longer needed."

Her failed attempt to pull back forced me to tighten my grasp. Now gripping the nape of her neck, I glared into her eyes and warned, "I dare you to try something...the entirety of your whole existence would be compromised."

CHAPTER FORTY-TWO

Cash: I Am My Mother's Child

I managed to place my emotions to the side long enough to put my final plan into motion. Although learning the truth about Vic's murder caught me off guard, it also added more fuel to the burning fire. I had to keep myself in check. I knew that if I made one mistake, it could jeopardize everything. I had taken more "L's" than I cared to admit. Tonight would give me some much needed gratification, to say the least. What I was feeling internally was beyond off-putting.

By the time Ev returned with everything on my list, I had just enough time to set up and get the ball rolling. I lit the candles one-by-one, creating the perfect ambiance for this special occasion. Tonight would qualify as one of those times when I had to look my absolute best and most seductive.

I dressed in a sexy teddy by La Perla, designed with black lace and satin ribbons. It accentuated every curve of my feminine figure. Brains had no knowledge of my incident. So to conceal my bruises, I wore a sexy dominatrix mask. Pleased with the results, I decided I might as well add a little role play to the agenda.

"Cash? Baby, where ya at?" the guest of honor bellowed, sending a sting of indignation throughout my body and spirit.

Pushing my ill thoughts to the background, I answered pleasantly. "In here, daddy!"

Brains strolled into the room, letting each well-placed rose petal guide him to the chair I had situated in the middle of my beautiful setting. "Damn, baby. You lookin'...and smellin' good," he whispered, pulling me into him. He kissed me softly, transferring some of my red lipstick onto his full lips.

"Have a seat," I ordered.

His eyes scanned the room as I backed up, using the remote to turn on *Beyoncé*'s "Drunk in Love." Brains nodded with eager expectancy as he inserted himself in the chair, slowly removing his button up. I handed him a double shot of Patrón and began serenading him with a song and special dance.

After a few minutes, I saw his eyes begin to grow heavy as his head bobbed back and forth, trying to stay alert. I gave him a bitter look of apathy, seeing that the Valium was quickly doing its job. It took less than ten minutes for his whole world to temporarily go black.

Muffled grunts and shuffling shook me out of my concentration. I glanced over at Brains' bound body and continued to proceed with caution. I fumbled around like a chemist with the battery acid I added to the water in the polypropylene bottle.

The muffled sounds of him coming to from the induced coma faded in and out. I remained attentive to the task before me. Finally satisfied with my concoction, I removed the thick, rubber gloves before standing erect.

I made my way over to him slowly and carefully, tilting my head to the side. I gave him an evil glare before raising my leg and lodging my black leather Tom Ford stiletto heel into his chest, forcing the chair back against the wall.

"The fuck is goin' on, Cash?"

I stood across from him as we locked eyes.

"Shhhh..." I said, pressing my finger against my lips. "Listen..." I pressed play on my phone and let the voicemail message play through the speaker. His eyes expanded to the size of saucers as he listened in disbelief. Pulling on leather gloves, I moved in silence.

"Cash, baby...it was an accident," he tried to explain as I moved closer.

I poured the acid onto his right leg. He let out a loud, pain-filled grunt. The acid ate right through his pants and continued to eat through his skin.

"Cash...baby, nooo...don't do this shit, girl," he begged.

I stood there unmoved, now ready to unveil the fundamental motive at hand. "I was there, Brains..."

His eyes widened in trepidation as I continued. I told him the story of my mother's murder, just as I remembered it. He sat in stunned silence and pain.

"Cash...you got it all wrong, baby," he babbled, shaking his head.

Not wanting to hear him utter another word, I tossed the battery acid onto his upper body, splattering his face. I watched and listened to him cry out in excruciating pain as the acid burned though his flesh and melted his facial features.

"Ahhhhh Cashmere! It burns, baby! Fuuuckkk!" he screamed as his body jerked.

I lit a cigarette, strictly for effect. I took a pull and enjoyed the scene. Before he could pass out from the pain, I put out my cigarette and recovered my pistol from my lace garter, aiming at his head.

"You're ju–st...as...vi–cious...as your fuc–kin' mo–ther..." he spat painfully with the exertion of each syllable.

I pulled the hammer back. "Well, I am my mother's child," I agreed, before pulling the trigger, sending a bullet through his skull.

I sent Natalia a quick "request for clean-up," text. Then, I planted the withered red rose he'd left in Meredith's casket onto his lifeless body. Finally, I made my exit, unhurried with poise and headed home to my man.

CHAPTER FORTY-THREE

Cashmere: Peace, Be Still

Two Months Later

I lay next to this man in tranquility. My mind was finally calm and serene now that my mission had been accomplished. I had no more tears left to cry when I envisioned the faces of Meredith and Vic, finally able to rest in peace. I was in harmony with myself and my past. I finally understood what they meant when they said, "*Peace, be still.*" I wanted to savor this feeling as long as possible.

"Cash, you sleep?"

My head rested on his chest while he stroked the side of my face. "Nah," I replied.

"What's wrong?"

I began drawing invisible lines and curves on his chest with my fingers. "I need to tell you something," I whispered.

For some reason, Slick was the only person that had ever seen me in such a susceptible state. He was the only man that I had ever truly loved since I was twelve years old. He taught me everything I knew when he finally realized that I was dead set on the brothel.

He even taught me how to build my empire without ever having to put in the work myself. Even though he wouldn't have dared teaching me how to fuck, I figured that one out on my own, enough to supersede the game.

Feeling safe with him, I decided to tell him the true nature of my relationship with Brains, the truth about that long ago day, and his murder, too. No one, and I mean no one, knew my true motives. I swallowed hard.

"Cash, you already know you can tell me anything. Shiddd, yo' ass wasn't hesitant to tell me when yo' damn period came. Now were you?"

I chuckled, remembering my twelve-year-old self tugging on Slick's hoodie, telling him to get me some pads from the store because I was a woman now.

"Yeah, and yo' ass was damn near 'bout to lock me up in the room and throw away the key, too," I teased.

"You damn right. It was either that or I was gone have to put some heat to every nigga that looked at you wrong."

The room fell silent as we lay there, reminiscing on the past with peaceful smiles on our faces. Finally, I exhaled, breaking the comfortable silence.

"I loved you so much then...and I love you even more today." This was the first time he heard me profess my love for him. I wasn't ashamed to let the sweet words escape from my lips.

Slick wrapped his arms around me and gave me a long, slow, passionate kiss before uttering the most beautiful words I'd ever heard. "Cashmere Jones, I have loved you from the moment I laid eyes on you. Being five years older didn't help my case, so I had to play that shit off to the best of my ability. I ain't wanna be no creep or no shit like that..."

I laughed. "Uh...well, creep sounds about right."

He tickled me all over my body, knowing damn well I hated that shit. I laughed uncontrollably until he pressed his lips onto mine, setting off all sorts of fireworks in my head and lower regions.

"I gotta tell you something, too..." he said, with a look of sincerity across his face.

I stared into his eyes, ready to take in whatever it was he had to say. "What's that?" I asked.

"A mufucka hungry, baby. Why don't you go make this creep some breakfast, before I turn you into a full entree?"

I raised my eyebrow, smacking my lips in playful annoyance. Then I gave him a lighthearted slap on the chest. He grabbed my wrists, bringing my hands up to his lips and kissing them.

"Then, I want you to tell me what it is that you been thinkin' about."

In full submission, I hopped out of the king-sized bed in my bra and boy shorts to oblige his request. I could feel his eyes deadlocked on me as my ass jiggled with every stride.

"I told you yo' ass was a creep," I said over my shoulder, before disappearing around the corner.

I stood over the stove, cooking breakfast and watching a few infomercials. I flipped through the channels, stopping on a news brief just in time.

> *"...police have discovered the body of thirty-year-old Leslie Davis. Davis was the daughter of newly appointed LAPD Commissioner Davis. The former Davis was reported missing forty-eight hours after the largest drug bust in U.S. history, which her father organized. Authorities have not yet confirmed if there is any connection between the two occurrences. Investigators are remaining tight lipped about the investigation. However, Commissioner Davis, the victim's father, has agreed to speak to KCAL 9 and CBS 2..."*

I sipped my coffee in contemplation as they showed paramedics transferring Leslie's body into the coroner's vehicle. I powered off the television in quiet contentment and went back to finishing breakfast. Putting the food onto plates, I paused as my phone did the Nae-Nae all across the countertop.

"Yeah..." I answered, placing the phone between my ear and shoulder for support.

"Cash, you in danger!" Aunt Judy warned.

Becoming instantly annoyed, I stopped what I was doing and leaned onto the kitchen counter. "What? What are you talkin' about?"

"Brains is dead, and you may be next..." she said, leaving a pregnant pause.

Vexed, I managed to pull it together, momentarily. "Why is that?" I asked out of habit.

"The hit on him was personal, Cash..."

"I know..."

"You know?" she snapped in confusion.

Taking a sip from my coffee, I continued. "Yeah...I know."

"How's that?" she pried.

"'Cause I killed 'im... Now you safe. You free, Judy. Alright? Damn!" I said, indignantly.

"Gal, what you go and do that for?"

Now, this woman was really starting to piss me off. "The hell you mean, 'what I do that for,' Judy? He killed Meredith...my mama, yo' sister—"

"Cashmere...nooo..." she interrupted.

My phone began beeping, signaling a low battery. This was one time I was glad my battery was gone die. "Look, I'm done talking..."

"You got it all wrong, Cash...Brains...he didn't kill Meredith..."

"Judy, stop protecting that man! It's over now," I hissed.

"Nah, it ain't. It's just beginning!" she yelled through the phone.

The aura in the room suddenly began to shift. I had no clue what was going on, but something didn't feel right. I realized why once I heard what discharged from her mouth, next. "Cash, baby..." she began, hesitantly. "Brains...didn't kill Meredith... That young boy, Slick, did... He—"

The sound of my phone powering off made me queasy. I turned around to see the love of my life, standing there behind me, quickly transforming into my biggest rival yet.

Evelyn: Cash Out!

My phone had been ringing all morning. Resigning myself to the fact that I wasn't going to be able to sleep in, I finally answered.

"You have a collect call from..."

"Azalea..."

"Azalea? Who the hell...?" I accepted the call, wondering who could be calling me from jail.

"Evelyn, it's Jersey."

My heart stopped momentarily. I was completely caught off guard. "Jersey? Girl, where the hell you been? Don't you know what's been going on out here?" I rambled.

"Ev, I was set up! I need you to reach out to your pops. I'm gonna need an attorney, asap!"

"What? Jers... Cash—"

"Evelyn, please! I can explain everything later. Just keep this shit between us, for now..."

I knew better than to go against Cash, but I was sure there must be a logical explanation behind everything. I never thought Jersey was in cahoots with the people who shot Cash, no way.

I took a deep breath. "Okay, Jersey. I'll get a hold of my papa, but first I need you to tell me everything."

The operator chimed in, disrupting our call.

"Evelyn, you need to hurry! Some mad shit's gonna go down in twenty-four hours, if I'm not out of here!"

Click!

Thank you so much for reading my book. If you enjoyed it, won't you please take a moment to leave me a review at your favorite retailer?

Thanks again!

Ty Nesha

ABOUT THE AUTHOR

Not afraid to let her imagination run wild, TyNesha also known as Sunshine, has done just that. Picking up a pen and allowing her words to lead the way as she tells the stories of her mind, has proven a cathartic method to relay the story of her life. It also enabled her to create a hard-hitting, contemporary, urban fictional tale, Cash Only: A Hoe Cartel, as the first installment of a three-part series depicting the lavish life of fast women, drug cartels, grisly murders, mad money, and erotic sexcapades while cruising the dark underbelly of Los Angeles.

We don't often get the opportunity to follow our dreams. However, TyNesha believes that if you want something, go for it! Turning her test into her incredible testimony is the main objective for her writing. Travel with her as she takes you on a captivating voyage through the depths of her mind each time she strokes a keyboard.

CPSIA information can be obtained
at www.ICGtesting.com
Printed in the USA
LVOW04s2014211016
509751LV00009B/981/P